SPECIAL MESSAGE TO READERS

This book is published under the auspices of

THE ULVERSCROFT FOUNDATION

(registered charity No. 264873 UK)

Established in 1972 to provide funds for research, diagnosis and treatment of eye diseases. Examples of contributions made are: —

A Children's Assessment Unit at Moorfield's Hospital, London.

•

Twin operating theatres at the Western Ophthalmic Hospital, London.

•

A Chair of Ophthalmology at the Royal Australian College of Ophthalmologists.

•

The Ulverscroft Children's Eye Unit at the Great Ormond Street Hospital For Sick Children, London.

You can help further the work of the Foundation by making a donation or leaving a legacy. Every contribution, no matter how small, is received with gratitude. Please write for details to:

THE ULVERSCROFT FOUNDATION,
The Green, Bradgate Road, Anstey,
Leicester LE7 7FU, England.
Telephone: (0116) 236 4325

In Australia write to:

THE ULVERSCROFT FOUNDATION,
c/o The Royal Australian and New Zealand College of Ophthalmologists,
94-98 Chalmers Street, Surry Hills,
N.S.W. 2010, Australia

THE GLOWING MAN

Under the cover of darkness and a violent storm, electrical engineer Sidney Cassell thought he'd committed the perfect murder. But immediately after pushing his rival to his death from atop a pylon, he himself is struck by a live high-voltage cable. Cassell survives the accident, only to discover that the electrical shock has affected his body strangely . . . Soon he becomes sucked into a vortex of murders and treachery, hunted by the police and unscrupulous scientists seeking the secret of his weird affliction.

Books by John Russell Fearn
in the Linford Mystery Library:

THE TATTOO MURDERS
VISION SINISTER
THE SILVERED CAGE
WITHIN THAT ROOM!
REFLECTED GLORY
THE CRIMSON RAMBLER
SHATTERING GLASS
THE MAN WHO WAS NOT
ROBBERY WITHOUT VIOLENCE
DEADLINE
ACCOUNT SETTLED
STRANGER IN OUR MIDST
WHAT HAPPENED TO HAMMOND?

JOHN RUSSELL FEARN

THE GLOWING MAN

Complete and Unabridged

LINFORD
Leicester

First published in Great Britain

First Linford Edition
published 2007

British Library CIP Data

Fearn, John Russell, *1908 – 1960*
The glowing man.—Large print ed.—
Linford mystery library
1. Electricity—Physiological effect—Fiction
2. Detective and mystery stories
3. Large type books
I. Title
823.9′12 [F]

ISBN 978–1–84617–600–5

Published by
F. A. Thorpe (Publishing)
Anstey, Leicestershire

Set by Words & Graphics Ltd.
Anstey, Leicestershire
Printed and bound in Great Britain by
T. J. International Ltd., Padstow, Cornwall

This book is printed on acid-free paper

1

The accident

The din of the storm was so overwhelming the two men could hardly hear each others' shouts as they worked with determined energy atop the three-hundred-foot high electric pylon. They were engaged on a service job — purely routine as far as they were concerned — but it demanded far more than just a sense of duty to grapple with the pylon in their efforts to repair the insulator which threatened to break and so drop the 100,000-volt feeder line.

'Higher up, Jim! Higher up!' Sidney Cassell bawled the words fiercely to the man above him — and Jim Prescott struggled further upwards, oilskins gleaming in the brief whiplash of lightning that seared the raging dark.

Sidney Cassell was the chief maintenance engineer of the line — tough, hardworking, never been known to shirk the most dangerous assignment, and this one was quite the deadliest yet. A slip or miscalculation and contact with the power line would be the prospect. After that, a short circuit down the pylon to earth, and that would be that.

It did seem to Jim Prescott, who could do naught else but obey orders, that Sid Cassell was miscalculating somewhere. Going higher up would not help things: it would simply make it more difficult to get down again. Just the same, Prescott continued to climb, glancing below now and again at the oil-skinned men watching the proceedings in searchlight beams from the ground.

'Okay!' Sid Cassell bawled at length, and Prescott held on tightly to the pylon crossbars, not a foot away from where the damaged insulator was creaking and rattling in the hurricane.

'What do I do?' he yelled. 'Do I fix it, or are you going to do it?'

'I'll do it,' Sid Cassell's voice floated up as he too began the ascent. Within a few seconds he had drawn himself level with Prescott.

A sense of uneasiness went through Jim Prescott. There was a curious expression on Sid's face as the lightning transiently revealed it. What could be seen of it between high-buttoned oilskin collar and sou'-wester was hard and merciless.

'You may not believe me,' Sid said bitterly, drawing himself up so that his face was close enough to Jim Prescott's for him to hear the words, 'but I've been waiting for a chance like this for months! We're up here alone. Jim — undisturbed! An accident would be considered the most natural thing in the world!'

Jim Prescott felt instinctively for the wrench in his belt.

'What the hell are you talking about, man?'

'I'm talking about Mary.'

A clap of thunder made the world vibrate for a moment and the faulty insulator rattled.

'Mary?' Prescott repeated. 'What the devil has she got to do with it? We're here to fix this insulator, not discuss our private lives — '

'We'll discuss as I see fit!' Sid's voice

was hard and flat. 'That we both happen to be in love with her is hard luck for one of us. You're not content to let her make her own choice. You've pushed yourself in every possible way — taken advantage of my every absence. But it's not going to go on that way, Jim! I'm going to settle the issue for myself, here and now!'

'Oh, stop talking like an idiot — !'

Jim Prescott pulled frantically at the wrench in his belt, but he was not quick enough. Sid's heavy boot came up, the point of the steel-shod shoe catching Prescott under the chin. It jolted him clean away from his grip on the crosspiece. He made one frantic lurch to save himself and then went reeling outwards into the dark. From below came shouts as the body hurtled into the midst of the assembled men.

Sid smiled crookedly to himself, and then shouted in apparent alarm. 'What happened? He lost his grip! How much hurt is he?'

'Looks like he's done for, Sid!' a cry floated back. 'Broken neck!'

Sid turned to the faulty insulator,

braced himself, then tugged out his wrench. With the methodical movements born of experience he set to work to make the repair, tightening up the massive bolts, engaging the clamps — then a sudden hurricane blast of the gale dislodged his grasp. It happened at the precise moment he was reaching towards the slack power wire.

He saw its long, dependent length come swinging straight at him, blown by the wind. Desperately he tried to dodge but it struck him full on and the universe seemed to explode into a fiery wilderness of pain and sparks.

After an interval of darkness, which could have been seconds or years, Sid Cassell became aware of visions. There seemed to be white-garbed figures, long vistas of darkness, mystic clinking sounds. Sometimes he glimpsed the familiar faces of Mary Carter and Fred Ashworth, the burly boss of the maintenance department.

Then, one day, all the strange little pieces in the jigsaw fitted into place and Sid realized that he was lying in bed in a hospital ward with Fred Ashworth regarding him. Further away stood Mary Carter. Hovering, watching with professional interest, was a doctor.

'Hello — boss,' Sid whispered.

'Take it easy, Sid,' Ashworth murmured, leaning forward. 'You're all right now. Nothing to get excited about. In case you don't know it — as of course you don't! — you're the world's miracle man! Everybody's talking about you.'

'About me?' Sid's voice was low from both exhaustion and surprise. 'Why, what did I do?'

'You absorbed a hundred thousand volts and lived to tell the tale! And nothing but a few trivial burns and two days unconsciousness to show for it.'

Sid thought it out drowsily and then he frowned. 'Did you say a hundred thousand volts? Couldn't be! You've got your wires crossed somewhere, boss.'

'No I haven't.' Ashworth shook his bullet head. 'I've had time to get all the facts. For some reason — and electricity is pretty funny stuff anyhow — you survived even after taking up the load when the power-feeder hit you. Ordinarily you ought to have become a crisp. That was just what the boys expected to find when they climbed up the pylon to get you. Instead you were just stunned and hanging by your safety belt. The doc says you'll make a good recovery — and you repaired that insulator. Good work, Sid! The Company won't forget you for it, believe me.'

'And Jim Prescott?' Sid asked, without opening his eyes.

The boss hesitated. 'Afraid it was just one of those things. He broke his neck when he fell from the pylon. Missed his hold, I gather?'

''Fraid so. I tried to grab him.'

Silence. Then at length Fred Ashworth stirred.

'Well, I'll be on my way. Just take it easy and report back for work when you get your discharge. 'Bye for now — and goodbye to you, Miss Carter,' Ashworth added pleasantly.

Sid opened his eyes again to find the girl looking at him. She looked just as pretty as ever — auburn hair peeping from under her saucy hat, a serious smile on her rose-tinted lips.

'Sid, dear . . . ' Her hand took his gently and her blue eyes searched his face. 'Please don't take it too hard about Jim. I know he was your best friend and — Well, the doctors said he must have died instantly. He didn't feel any pain or anything.'

'He didn't? That's fine.' Long pause. 'Just how do you feel about the accident?'

'I've accepted it by now. He was buried yesterday following the inquest. They recorded 'Death from Misadventure'. The shock is beginning to abate.'

'You liked him a lot, Mary — '

'We were good friends,' she admitted, sighing. 'But I like you a lot, too. I want to help you to get well again quickly.'

'Thanks, Mary. With you at the back of me I'm sure it won't take long.'

Nor did it. In three weeks Sid Cassell was back at work feeling none the worse for his experience — though at times he did wonder how he had absorbed 100,000 high-tension volts and escaped instant death. So much did the problem worry him he finally searched the reference library for some parallel case to his own, and ultimately landed on an instance which made him realize he was not entirely unique. There was, for instance, the case of Elizabeth Drew, who in 1932 was struck by a flash of lightning estimated at eight million volts. She survived with nothing worse than a momentary dizziness and a two-day loss of memory. So perhaps his own experience had not been so fantastic after all.

Being an electrician, though, it did seem to him that that huge voltage must have gone somewhere. He had been told that when the power wire had struck him lights had dipped over a wide area, so there had certainly been some kind of short circuit.

As week succeeded week and no plausible solution occurred to him, he gradually forgot all about the incident, continuing his work as chief maintenance engineer and spending his spare time with Mary. They were both agreed that they should become engaged in the late spring and marry in the summer.

'There's a chance I may get promotion,' Sid told her, as they sat together in the park late one warm spring evening. 'The boss has already hinted at it. If it does come off we'll be on velvet.'

The girl nodded, staring absently into the twilight. The air was as warm as early summer — deceptively so. Winter might yet return in all its fury and Sid might once again find himself wrestling with death atop some swaying pylon.

'I've been thinking,' Mary said presently, turning. 'If we get engaged in — '

Then she stopped. Abruptly, completely, like a radio switched off. Sid glanced at her in wonder.

'If we get engaged?' he repeated. 'No doubt about it, is there?'

'Sid, look at yourself!' the girl ordered, fascinated.

'Huh?' In surprise he glanced down, and then gave a start. Though the twilight had now deepened to near night, he could see his hands! Not actually *as* hands, but as dim red outlines, glowing as a slightly heated poker glows in a dark room.

'What the devil — !' he exclaimed,

jumping up and staring at his fingers. 'What's happened to them?'

'Your face is the same!' Mary cried, horrified. 'It's — it's awful!'

Quickly she fumbled in her handbag and brought out a mirror, handing it over. Incredulously Sid gazed at himself. It looked for all the world as though his face were in the glow of a crimson spotlight!

'I never saw anything like it,' he said at length, and his voice was shaken as he strove to master an over-riding fear. 'It looks as if I'm on fire, or something! Yet I feel all right. Not hot or anything.'

'You'd better go and see a doctor right away,' Mary said uneasily, taking the mirror back. 'I'll go with you as far as the end of the road and then — '

'Far as the end of the road!' Sid glared at her in the gloom. 'What you mean is you don't want to be seen with me like this!'

'Can you blame me? Be reasonable, Sid! It's frightening!'

'You go,' he said brusquely. 'I'll look after myself.'

Without hesitation Mary took him at

his word. She was mortally scared, even though she had not openly admitted it. Sid watched her go into the dark, then he took another look at his reddish-glowing hands and finally pushed them into his jacket pockets. He could not understand what had gone wrong, but he did know that no doctor was likely to have the necessary knowledge to make a diagnosis. This was not a medical problem: it seemed electrical, and the one man likely to have a solution was Frank Billings, chief engineer at the powerhouse.

His mind made up, Sid went down all the quiet back streets and arrived in the droning powerhouse some twenty minutes later. Frank Billings, the chief, and an expert electrician if ever there was one, was contemplating the central meter-board when Sid arrived. Frank Billings glanced towards him and waved a hand in greeting.

'Hello there, Sid! Love your work so much you come to it in your spare time?'

Sid hesitated. The perfectly natural greeting made him realize that there could not be anything unusual about his appearance. Stealthily he drew his hands out of his pockets and looked at them. Here in the bright overhead lights they had quite a normal aspect.

'It's not that,' he said, advancing until he was facing the engineer. 'There's something worrying me — an electrical problem, and I think you're the man to help me. Mind if we go into your office for a moment?'

'Surely.' Billings motioned to an engineer to take over and then led the way down the center aisle. Sid followed him into the office and closed the door.

'Take a look at this,' he said quietly, and switched off the light

In the darkness he immediately became visible, glowing with somber red fire about the face and hands. The effect only ceased where his clothes intervened. A long, low whistle of amazement escaped the chief engineer.

'Sweet balls of fire, Sid, what's happened to you?'

The lights came up again and Sid smiled morosely. 'That's what I want to find out. Any suggestions?'

Billings pondered through a long interval and then shook his head.

'Afraid I haven't. I never saw anything like it before. Only thing I can suggest is that it's some sort of hangover from that electric shock you got recently. Maybe it's worked in something like the same way that radium-poisoning works. Your skin has become phosphorescent.'

Sid frowned and shook his head. 'It's something more than that, I'm sure. Only I'm not scientist enough to be able to figure it out. I thought that you perhaps, understanding electricity so well, might have some solution.'

'Sorry. All I can suggest is that you wait and see how it goes on, and if any ideas occur to me I'll let you know.'

Sid nodded moodily, reflected for a moment, then with a sigh he left the office. Billings ambled to the office door and watched the tall, lean figure disappear through the powerhouse's main entrance.

'Of all the impossible things,' Billings whispered, a fascinated look in his eyes. 'And the poor mug doesn't see for himself what's happened.'

He wasted no further time. He gave one swift check-over to the whining electrical dynamos, left instructions with the second-engineer, and then departed in his car to the residence of Denham Roberts, the President of the International Power and Light Combine.

The big man was at home, but by no means pleased at being disturbed. Had it been anybody else but the chief engineer there would have been no admittance.

'Sorry for the intrusion, sir,' Billings apologized, as he came into the library, where Roberts was in an easy chair, reading. 'I have discovered something which I think will do us a lot of good if we act quickly — and carefully.'

Roberts — short, thick-set, his velvet jacket drawn taut over his bulging stomach, got to his feet.

'Meaning what?' he asked briefly.

'I believe, sir, that I can lay my hands on the formula for something which scientists have sought for generations. In other words — cold light.'

Denham Roberts was not a scientist as

such, but even he knew that the one bugbear of all lighting systems is the amount of heat, and consequent wear and tear, produced. His eyes sharpened immediately.

'Cold light, eh? Whose discovery is it?'

'Hardly a discovery, sir. An accident. I've seen a living demonstration of cold light tonight, in its incipient stages, anyhow.'

'You are quite sure it *is* cold light?'

Billings shrugged. 'I don't pretend to be a great scientist, Mr. Roberts, but even *I* know that when visible light fails to give off any heat it's something vastly important, particularly in our line of business. At present this light is only at the red end of the scale and for that reason it should radiate quite a deal of heat — but it doesn't.'

'Have a drink,' Roberts invited abruptly, and went over to the cocktail cabinet. When he had poured the drinks and brought them back he asked briefly, 'What the devil are you talking about?'

'I'm talking about Sidney Cassell, our chief maintenance engineer. He belongs, as I do, to United Power Lines, of which you are the President, along with other companies. Not very long ago he got a hundred-thousand volt boost and now it seems to have developed into a 'disease', if you can call it that. I'll stake all my electrical knowledge on the fact that if you can get him to submit to a scientific examination, preferably without him knowing it, you'll find he's taken unto himself the secret of cold light. That secret, transferred to lamps, could net a fortune.'

'Yes,' Roberts agreed, his drink forgotten in his hand. 'Yes, it definitely could.'

'In the past,' Frank Billings finished, 'I've given you many worthwhile tips, for a consideration. This is another one — also for a consideration.'

'And suppose you are wrong?'

'If I am, then I get no pay. Nothing could be fairer than that. But if I am right, as I'm convinced I am, there is a fortune just around the corner. All we need is a physicist, or a group of them, to examine Sid Cassell.'

Roberts made up his mind and then

finished his drink.

'Give me the details, then we can get some action.'

* * *

Sid Cassell returned to his city apartment in a grim mood. The first fright he had received at the discovery of his extraordinary 'ailment' had gone now and instead he was more inclined to try and analyze what had happened to him. He was thankful for the fact that he lived alone; it would give him the chance to experiment without having to answer a variety of difficult questions. Also he would be able to dodge a great deal of unwelcome publicity.

The first test he made was with a voltmeter, but it registered zero when he took it in both hands. That seemed to indicate that he was not electrically haywire. Next he took his temperature and found it normal. In fact he did everything he could think of, including the recording of his heartbeats and reflexes, neither of which was abnormal.

At length he had a meal, pondered obscurely on the problem, and so finally went to bed. The moment he had switched off the light he could see his hands lying on the coverlet like glowing, ruby-tinted gloves.

'All right, glow!' he muttered impatiently. 'What the hell do I care? I feel okay, so what does it matter anyhow?'

That he said such things purely because he was scared silly he knew full well, so with an effort he switched his thoughts to Mary. It had come to him as rather a shock to discover how rapidly she had dropped him the moment he had become 'peculiar'. Couldn't altogether blame her, of course, but he had always thought that women liked the job of helping a man through a crisis. Perhaps she did not really love him at all, then, and was just making do with him as a second best to Jim Prescott. The memory of Jim Prescott tightened Sid's lean jaw for a moment and he lived again that incident at the top of the pylon when he had hurled Jim to his death.

'He got in the way anyhow,' Sid

growled, and then he set about the task of forcing himself to sleep.

Though he succeeded he slumbered only fitfully and when he finally woke it was still dark. He looked tardily at his hands, hoping inwardly he would discover that he had dreamed the whole thing — but no, they were still glowing, and now there seemed to be a faintly yellowish tinge creeping into the red.

For a long time he debated as to whether he should report for work or not. After all, this strange defect did not show in daylight, and indeed nobody knew of it at all except Frank Billings and Mary. Perhaps it would be as well to turn in — but what if he was sent on an assignment that might extend into the dark hours? He would have to try and answer all kinds of complicated questions.

By the time he had shaved and dressed he had come to a decision. He picked up the telephone and got through to Mary Carter's rooming house. After a while she answered him.

'Hello there, Sid!' Her voice sounded anxious. 'How are you getting on? Did you find out what went wrong last night?'

'No I didn't — but I will. I'm going to the hospital this morning to see the doctor who pulled me through the electric shock I got. Maybe he will be able to help — '

'You mean you're still — er — Well, I can't say it over the 'phone in case anybody is listening to me, but you know what I mean.'

'Yes, I know what you mean, and I'm still the same only not quite so red. Frankly, I'll be hanged if I can understand it. Look, Mary, I rang you up to see if we can fix up a fresh date. I want to talk with you — '

'While you're like that!'

'I can cover my face with a scarf and wear gloves. I won't show then. Mary, don't walk out on me now, please. You're the only person I can talk to!'

'Maybe so, but I can't stand even looking at you while you're like that. Just forget all about me until you've recovered. Sorry, Sid, but I'm sure that's the best way.'

The line clicked and Sid stared blankly;

then he slammed the telephone down onto its cradle.

'Of all the cheap, shabby, low-down — ' His mouth set harshly. He was just beginning to comprehend the fact that Mary Carter was not really worth attention at all: she was too selfish. In that case he had wiped out Jim Prescott and become an unconvicted murderer all for nothing.

Grim-faced, he went and gathered together some breakfast, ate it, and then relying on the daylight to camouflage his malady he took a taxi to the hospital and, towards two o'clock, saw the doctor who had attended him during his recovery from electric shock. The medico listened in silence, frowning, and at the end of the story he drew down he window blinds and contemplated the yellowish-red face and hands looming in oddly disembodied luminescence before him.

'This,' he said, releasing the blinds again, 'runs into a branch of science which goes far beyond medicine. If you'll wait a moment, Mr. Cassell, I'll have a word with Dr. Craymond of the Electro-Physical Laboratory. He might be able to help us. He's advised me on many an electrical victim.'

'Thanks,' Sid muttered, and sat down to listen detachedly as the physician 'phoned for the scientist to come over.

Bruce Craymond, when he arrived, proved to be a small, intensely thoughtful man. In total silence he listened to the details as both Sid and the doctor gave them; then he too studied Sid in the again darkened room.

'And your entire body is like this, Mr. Cassell?' he asked, when daylight had been restored.

'All over, yes.'

'And last night you say the tint was redder than it is now? There was less yellow in it?'

'That's right.'

'And recently you got a shock of a hundred thousand volts, and survived it?'

'Correct.'

The physicist stroked the side of his jaw with one finger and reflected. Finally he turned to the physician.

'Have you taken our young friend's temperature, doctor?'

'No, but I can soon do so — '

'Don't bother,' Sid interrupted. 'Everything is normal — heart, temperature, and reflexes. I know enough to test them for myself . . . Look, Dr. Craymond, you're a scientist so what's the answer? I want it straight.'

Craymond hesitated. 'The answer is so amazing I hardly know how to give it, Mr. Cassell. It's so — fantastic! Yet, all other things being equal I don't see how I can be wrong. I believe, young man, that you have fortuitously accomplished a scientific miracle! Instead of absorbing radiation you are *reflecting* it, at a higher wavelength than is normal.'

Sid frowned and gave both men a puzzled glance.

'It's like this,' Craymond continued. 'This world of ours is saturated night and day by all manner of radiations, but in particular by cosmic rays, the name we have for ultra short radiation pouring in from outer space. That much you will know for yourself — or should. Normally we absorb these cosmic rays and very slightly reflect them, but of course they are reflected invisibly. We neither see or feel them. The reason for that, and this fact is applicable to either an organic or inorganic body, is that the molecules are not excited enough to give off radiation of a wavelength between 0.00004 and 0.00008 centimetres, which comprises the visible spectrum.

'A certain amount of heat is generated in the impact of course, because the kinetic energy of the radiation is transferred to the molecules and they are excited accordingly. But you are not a normal organic subject, Mr. Cassell, in that you recently received and survived a shock of one hundred thousand volts.'

'That's right,' Sid admitted, pondering. 'I've tried to imagine what happened when that current surged through me.'

'What happened is now self-evident, young man. Every molecule in your body underwent a violent conversion. The molecules, if you will, received a terrific boost, the effect of which is only just becoming apparent. This effect is, that instead of absorbing cosmic radiation in the normal way, as everybody and everything does, you reflect it back as visible light at the lower end of the spectrum — the red end. And why? Because your molecules are reacting at a speed infinitely greater than normal. The vibration of a molecule, and that includes the atomic set-up within it, determines whether or not it is the visible or invisible spectrum.'

Sid groped in a mental darkness for a while. 'You — you mean that instead of reflecting a low order of invisible heat radiations, caused by kinetic energy when cosmic rays strike my molecules, I'm reflecting them in a higher order instead, as visible light?'

'That's it.' Craymond looked quite delighted. 'You are transforming invisible energy into radiant light. There is no difference between light and heat radiation as such, remember; they both travel at one hundred and eighty six thousand miles a second, but the different wavelengths determine the visibility thereof, or otherwise. Naturally, since cosmic rays are with us night and day you also react night and day. Your body has been transformed into a chemical laboratory, in much the same way as plants draw in carbon dioxide and give off oxygen in return.'

'Should there be heat?' Sid asked, mystified.

'Why? Your molecules are vibrating at the wavelength that gives *light*, therefore there can't be heat; not appreciable heat, anyway. All you have is your normal bodily temperature — the kinetic value of change created by digestive processes. The other state, cosmic ray transmission, normally absorbed and unnoticed, is reflected as pure light — steady light. In fact,' Craymond finished, a strange look in his eyes, 'cold light!'

Sid gave the slightest of starts. He was an electrician and he knew exactly what cold light implied.

'It all sums up to the fact that I'm a sort of human glow-worm?' he asked.

'Most certainly not!' Craymond looked offended. 'Glow-worm indeed! You are infinitely more complex than the glow-worm. The glow-worm merely utilizes the basic elements of phosphorescence, which gives off light previously absorbed. You are a human transformer, emanating cosmic radiation as pure cold light without heat — a natural phenomenon that men have struggled for ages to find. Light without heat!'

Sid gave a sigh. 'I'm not a bit impressed by becoming a phenomenon, Dr. Craymond. How do I put myself *right*? That is what's worrying me!'

'That's something I can't tell you,' the physicist confessed, musing. 'In fact your condition bothers me quite a lot. First you converted radiation at the red end of the spectrum, and during the few hours that have elapsed since it started it has become yellowish. That is the second stage of the visible spectrum. Then comes blue and finally violet, as the molecular activity becomes swifter and the wavelength shorter.'

There was a long silence; then for Sid at least the staggering truth seemed to sink in somewhat. As it did so he gave a little gasp.

'Great heavens, Dr. Craymond, you're

not suggesting surely that my molecules are going to keep up this devil's dance until I disintegrate at the top end of the spectrum scale?'

'I am a scientist,' Craymond replied quietly. 'Personal considerations for your fate do not concern me. All I do know is that your molecular make-up has been started on an intense vibratory path by the original hundred-thousand volt shock you got, and that these molecules are already excited enough to show red light where none should be. I cannot see why the process should stop, particularly as you have gone from the red to the yellow wavelength. For your sake I hope the trouble subsides. Scientifically, it is possible that the molecules, in striving to find a new balance, will creep up the scale until . . . Well, I would prefer not to discuss that.'

'I demand that you do!' Sid snapped. 'This is *me* you are talking to! I'm the poor devil who's in danger. There has got to be some scientific way of curing me!'

'There is only one way, and you can do it yourself. Find some method of covering yourself with lead sheathing. That will block you from cosmic rays and may give you a chance to revert to normal, and thereby survive. Better still,' Craymond added, 'come to the Electro-Physical Laboratory this afternoon and I'll arrange something. We'll keep you under observation and see what can be done. In the meantime remember that you are worth at least ten million, and probably more.'

'Ten million? Pounds do you mean? But why?'

'Dammit, man, haven't I told you?' Craymond exclaimed. 'Cold light! That's worth ten million of any investor's money! If only whatever has happened to you can be duplicated in inanimate matter, to make it transmit cold light instead of kinetic heat energy, it will bring in a new era. Just keep on remembering that you are worth ten million, and protect yourself. I'll see after examining you if the Electro-Physical Laboratory would be prepared to pay you the sum I've mentioned for permission to duplicate the peculiarity governing you . . . You come along this afternoon and we'll see what we can do.'

'Right.' Sid gave a somewhat dazed nod and rose to his feet. 'And thanks for the diagnosis, doctor, staggering though it is.'

2

Wanted man

Sid Cassell left the hospital in a thoughtful mood. Now the cause of the trouble had been explained to him it did not seem half so terrifying. The biggest surprise of all had been to discover that he had suddenly become worth ten million of 'any investor's money.' Ten million! And with lead sheathing he might still survive and be ten million the richer for his astonishing experience. Yes, it was a situation which definitely needed consideration.

And it was as he strolled along the footpath in the bright sunlight that he began to realize that a smooth, long black car was gutter-crawling beside him. A voice suddenly hailed him.

'Cassell! Cassell, just a minute!'

Sid stopped and turned, surprised to find himself looking at the bulldog face of

Denham Roberts peering above the car's opened rear window.

'Mr. Roberts!' Sid exclaimed, moving to the kerb as the oar stopped. 'What has the President of the Power Combine in common with a maintenance engineer that he has to follow him around?'

'Plenty,' Roberts answered. 'Else I wouldn't do it. You have had me worried, Cassell. I left word at your depot this morning that I wanted you to report personally to me. When you didn't show up I had my boys trace you, and it led to the hospital. Hop in. I want a word with you.'

Sid hesitated for a moment, then with a shrug he climbed into the car and settled in the luxurious upholstery. In a moment the car was on its way again and Denham Roberts sat breathing heavily and looking out of the window.

'How would you like to work for me exclusively?' he asked, as though Sid were not even present.

'Why should I? I'm doing all right as a maintenance engineer.'

'And risking your neck time after time.

Don't tell me you really enjoy it! You can't be so much in love with your job, otherwise you'd have turned in this morning. I heard all about that hundred-thousand-volt kick you got, you know. If you were to work for me exclusively there'd be no such risk. I'd put you in an executive position and the days of climbing power pylons would be over. I don't know exactly what the department pays you, but it would still be trebled and tax free.'

'Which means there's something funny somewhere,' Sid replied, his voice grim. 'You, the President of an enormous combine, seek me out personally to offer me a good job, and all you know about me is that I'm a maintenance engineer.'

'I know the men who work for me, Cassell,' Roberts turned at last and looked at Sid directly. 'Besides, I feel that you are entitled to some recompense for the fine job you did on the night of the storm.'

'A combine does not have a heart, sir,' Sid responded. 'Nor does its President.'

'Stop talking like a fool, man! I'm

offering you a first-class chance — '

'Maybe, but I don't want it. If you want me it will cost you a cool ten million, tax free. I've got it into my head that your only reason for wanting me is to analyze me from head to foot. I have no doubt but that whilst I work you will have scientists rig up all manner of devices to find out what makes me tick. You're not looking for an executive; you're looking for the secret of cold light and you are reasonably sure that I've got it, imprisoned inside me! I know I have, because a physicist at the hospital told me so, though how you found out I can't imagine. Unless — ' Sid's eyes narrowed. 'Unless Frank Billings! Yes, why not? He's a smart man, and the only one to whom I showed myself.'

There was no expression on Roberts's face — unless a fixed kind of smile could be called an expression.

'All right, so I want you for the analysis of cold light,' he admitted. 'That you know the reason doesn't make my offer invalid. I was merely trying to spare you the — er — embarrassment of examination by scientists.'

'Kind of you,' Sid retorted. 'I'm not in the market. And this is where I get off.'

'As you wish.' Roberts spoke into the phone at his side and the limousine halted. Sid opened the door and stepped out onto the footpath, turning back as Roberts spoke again.

'I hope you won't have reason to regret this, Cassell.'

'I shan't. And thanks for the ride!' Sid slammed the door and turned into the midst of the people thronging the pavement. Roberts sat motionless for a moment or two and then gave his chauffeur further instructions.

'To my office. Quickly.'

Meanwhile Sid made his way back to his apartment. Reaching it he whipped up the telephone and rang the hospital, by which means he ultimately got in touch with Dr. Craymond.

'Oh yes, Mr. Cassell!' the physicist exclaimed, as though a light had dawned. 'What's the trouble?'

'Trouble in plenty I'm afraid. A

colleague of mine has opened his mouth wider than he should and told the President of the Power and Light Combine that I'm 'potted cold light'. I've just had a brush with the President as it is. I wiped him down, but I'm not fool enough to think it will stop at that. I'm in need of protection, so I consider it's the responsibility of the Electro-Physical Laboratory to see that I get it. You mentioned the figure of ten million for the pleasure of analyzing me.'

'True — but that could only come after consultation with the directors, Mr. Cassell. I think you — '

'Unless you act quickly and send an escort to bring me to you I don't guarantee you'll ever see me again.' Sid paused significantly. 'I've set a light to an atom bomb this morning and it may explode at any moment.'

'I quite understand,' Craymond replied quickly. 'I'll do all I can. Meantime stay right where you are. You are much too valuable to be walking around loose.'

'So I've discovered!' Sid put the 'phone back on its cradle and then prepared himself to wait, meanwhile wondering what the temporarily baulked president of the Power Combine would do next.

In actual fact Roberts, back in his office, was doing plenty. Before him, summoned specially for the purpose, stood Frank Billings, chief of the powerhouse.

'Overture number one to our overloaded friend has failed, Billings,' Roberts said briefly. 'Unfortunately he already knows what is the matter with him, so he forestalled me — '

'But you didn't let him go, surely!' Billings exclaimed. 'Now he's wise to the situation he'll — '

'Let me speak, will you?' Roberts demanded. 'I couldn't do anything then — not in a crowded main street. I wouldn't be such a fool . . . The point is he'll be on the lookout now for anything I may try to pull, so some of my boys chasing after him just won't do. I sent for you to find out a few things about him. What friends has he? Friends who might be bought to play the game our way if paid sufficiently.'

Billings reflected. 'Only close friend be had was Jim Prescott, and he took a tumble and finished himself. Nobody else he'd trust — unless it's Mary Carter.'

'Ah!' A gleam came into the big man's close-set eyes. 'So there is a woman in it, is there? What are the prospects?'

'That I can't say. I've been introduced to her and she struck me as pretty much the self-seeking type.'

'All to the good. Know her address?'

'No — but I've seen the house where she has rooms. I walked that far one evening with Cassell and Jim Prescott — and Mary as well, of course.'

'Then go and find her. If she's at business find out where that is and get her. I've got to have her immediately. I know this is right out of your normal routine, but the emergency demands it. We can't afford to let Cassell slip through our fingers.'

'I agree there,' Billings said, 'but what are you planning to do with the girl?'

'Leave that to me. Hurry up, man. Every moment counts.'

So Frank Billings departed, on his

quite unanticipated errand. About which time Sid was still waiting anxiously in his apartment . . . and at the Electro-Physical Laboratory Dr. Craymond was in conference with Sir Devenish Rondel, the famous physicist who ruled the equally famous organization.

'I'm afraid it's out of the question, Dr. Craymond,' he decided, when the scientist had finished speaking. 'To provide an escort for this man Cassell, just because you have developed an extraordinary theory about him, is quite outside my jurisdiction. I wouldn't dare make a decision without the backing of the full quorum of directors.'

'But — this is an emergency!' Craymond insisted, as though the statement covered everything.

Sir Devenish gave a tolerant smile. 'Only from your own point of view, Dr. Craymond. I have to remind you that many times in the past your theories have been proven somewhat — ah — untenable, which is one good reason for my hesitancy at the moment.'

'I tell you this man is the embodiment

of cold light! I know he is! He's there for the asking, and we can take the biggest stride yet in science as far as light is concerned. If we don't somebody else will, maybe with unpleasant consequences for our young friend.'

'I am afraid, Dr. Craymond, that if Mr. Cassell requires protection he must apply to the police. I have no objection to your making an examination of him, if he is willing, and should there be convincing proof of your theory of cold light then we'll go further — but I cannot do anything more. He must come of his own volition. We cannot possibly undertake to be responsible for his safety . . .'

And with that Dr. Craymond had to be satisfied. He returned to his own particular department in the physical laboratory and went into his office, picking up the telephone. In a few moments he was speaking to an obviously worried Sid Cassell

'Very well then,' Sid said, when he heard the decision. 'I'll have to take the risk for myself and come over. I'd better do it right away before the Power

Combine president has time to do anything. Wish I'd known earlier. I've given him the opportunity to get organized.'

'I'll expect you as soon as possible,' Craymond replied, 'and if you feel like asking for police protection it's up to you.'

'I wouldn't get it. The basis of my fear is all too flimsy. Besides, it might involve my explaining my condition and that I don't intend to do. I'll be with you as quickly as I can.'

Sid rang off and, though definitely chary about the risk he was taking, he turned to the door. He had it half open when the telephone rang. For a moment he hesitated. It seemed the most sensible idea to ignore it with so much urgency motivating him . . . On the other hand it might be something of unexpected importance. He returned to it in a couple of strides and yanked it up.

'Yes? Sidney Cassell speaking.'

'Hello, Sid. This is Mary.'

'Oh,' Sid muttered, not quite sure what to say. 'Anything wrong?'

'I've become conscience-stricken, Sid. I realize I treated you pretty badly this morning when you rang up.'

'No use me denying it,' he responded. 'You certainly did.'

The girl's voice went on quickly. 'I want to make it up, Sid. I didn't feel so good this morning when I woke up, which is perhaps why I acted so badly. I want particularly to know how you got on at the hospital. When can we meet, and fix up that new date you were referring to?'

'Sure you mean this?' Sid asked suspiciously.

'Of course I mean it! I wouldn't be ringing up otherwise, would I? I'm 'phoning from work, in case you're wondering. Look, I've an early lunch here today — eleven thirty. How about meeting me at the *Mimosa Café*?'

'Afraid it can't be done,' Sid answered. 'I've an extremely urgent appointment I must keep right away — '

'Oh, all right, if that's how you feel about it! Don't expect me to ever eat humble pie again, that's all. Goodbye.'

'No — no, just a moment!' Sid glanced at his watch and thought swiftly. He just could not allow Mary to slip away when she had come back of her own accord. 'I'll postpone my appointment. It was originally for this afternoon so I'll put it back again to that. See you at the *Mimosa* in ten minutes. How's that?'

'I'll be there!' Mary responded promptly, and rang off.

Sid reflected for a moment, then dialed swiftly In a matter of moments he had put off Dr. Craymond until the afternoon, to that scientific gentleman's vague astonishment. This done, Sid felt satisfied. That he would take a risk in lunching with Mary at the *Mimosa Café* he knew full well, but it seemed worth it in order to cling onto her — and plainly it could be done no other way.

So, presently he set off using all the alleyways and minor streets he could in order to reach his destination. He arrived without mishap and thereafter spent an anxious five minutes window-gazing until Mary should show up. When eventually she did so she regarded him in surprise.

‘Why the crouching walk?’ she inquired. ‘You look as if you’re hiding from the police, or something!’

‘I’m hiding from something just as bad,’ he replied, taking her arm. ‘Let’s get in the café and then I’ll explain.’

He hurried her quickly into the café’s fairly quiet interior and made for a corner table. He took care, nonetheless, that it was close to a window, the light through which negated any possibility of his own queer luminescence being visible. When he had given the order Mary gave him another questioning look.

‘What did you mean about ‘hiding’?’ she asked.

Briefly Sid explained; then he gave a grateful smile. ‘All else apart though, Mary, I’d take any risk to keep a date with you. You don’t know how much it means to me to have you clear up the little difficulty of this morning. Everything seemed to close up on me when you cut me off on the ’phone.’

‘Sorry,’ she muttered, averting her eyes. ‘Just the way I felt as I told you. But even now, if we’re to be seen together at night,

I think you should take certain precautions. I hardly want to be seen walking around with a sort of — of glorified Roman Candle. Besides, it couldn't obtain. You'd have the authorities after you, and me, too. All right in the daytime, but — You *do* understand, don't you?'

'Of course,' Sid smiled. 'And until this queer business is over we'll meet only in the daylight hours. Maybe each day at lunchtime like this? How's that?'

'Just right,' Mary agreed; then quickly, 'And what did they say at the hospital? What *is* the matter with you?'

'I hardly think you'd understand even if I told you. It's long, involved, and scientific. But at least it has one advantage for both of us. It's turned me into a potential millionaire.'

There was a pause as the waitress brought the lunch; then Mary hunched forward eagerly. 'A potential millionaire? But in what way? You don't mean going on view as a freak, or something, do you? I'd hardly like my husband-to-be doing that — '

'Nothing like that. I'd become an

exhibit, yes, but only for scientists, entirely because I have unexpectedly developed the phenomenon know as cold light. That is why I'm so scared of Denham Roberts and his mob trying to nab me.'

'So *that's* the reason?' Mary frowned to herself. 'What in the world is cold light, anyway?'

It took Sid the rest of the lunchtime to try to explain. And even then he doubted if the unscientific Mary understood a word of what he had said.

'Anyway,' he finished, 'it means that when I do finally get myself sorted out we ought to be on velvet. I may have to wear a peculiar sort of suit for a while to get myself right, but that's a small thing weighed against ten million pounds.'

Mary nodded but she did not say anything. She seemed to be lost in thought — or so Sid imagined. He paid the lunch check and escorted her out of the café — then he glanced up in surprise as four well-dressed, powerfully-built men mysteriously appeared and closed around him and the girl.

'Just keep walking, Mr. Cassell,' one of them said. 'You won't get hurt if you do. Go to that car at the kerb there.'

Sid clenched his fists and glanced around him sharply, but the men had contrived it so neatly there was no way out — most certainly not with the bulge of an automatic in at least two pockets.

'With the compliments of Denham Roberts, I suppose?' Sid demanded bitterly.

'That's it,' assented the spokesman. 'No use blaming us, Mr. Cassell: we're only obeying orders. All right, Miss Carter, you've done your part. You can go.'

'Done your — ?' Sid stared at Mary as she quickly wriggled away and hurried into the midst of the passers-by. 'Look here, do you mean *she* deliberately arranged all this?'

'Looks that way,' answered the spokesman laconically. 'Get a move on, will you? We haven't all day!'

Sid had no alternative, though he did wonder for a brief moment if he mightn't risk everything in making a dash for it. The men would hardly fire after him in the open street, but they'd certainly get him later if they didn't do it now, so there seemed little point in toughening the issue.

His face set with angry resentment, far more against Mary than the men who were merely doing a job, Sid dropped into the rear of the car and there sat in silence as he was whisked through the city streets and, finally, to the section of the Power and Light Combine that he knew comprised the private and general laboratories.

In fact from here on he was on quite familiar ground, until his march through the corridors ended at a laboratory marked 'Private'. Here he had never been before: it was the sacrosanct territory of Denham Roberts himself.

Sure enough Roberts was present, and with him were half a dozen men whom, from their appearance, Sid judged to be members of the scientific profession. One of them he even recognized — Grimsby Tate, an electronic scientist who had recently been dismissed from his post in a Government undertaking because of questionable activity with a foreign power. If the rest of the men were in such bad odor as Tate the future did not seem very bright.

'Sorry to have to appeal directly to force, Mr. Cassell, but there was no other way,' Roberts explained, as Sid was released from his captors' grip and advanced. 'Only yourself to blame, you know. I offered you a sporting chance this morning and you turned me down. Now I'm not offering anything. I'm going to take what I want — or rather these scientists are. You've been a bit of a fool, haven't you?'

'How much has Mary Carter to do with this?' Sid asked deliberately.

Roberts grinned round his cigar. 'Practically everything, bless her! Just shows, Cassell, you can't trust a woman — not Mary Carter's sort anyway. For the trifling thousands I offered her she was quite prepared to deliver me your head on a charger, or a reasonable facsimile. However, we are wasting time. I'm handing you over to the scientists, Mr. Cassell, and the rest is up to them. We'll meet later.'

With that Roberts departed. Sid looked after him, then back to the scientists, and afterwards to the four strong-arm men who were still ready for action if need be.

'Don't think you're going to be killed, Mr. Cassell,' Grimsby Tate said, grinning cynically. 'You wouldn't be any use dead; your cold light effect would die with you. All we want to do — and are going to do — is analyze you in detail. Now strip whilst we prepare.'

'Damned if I will,' Sid retorted.

'If you won't you'll stay around until sheer hunger and thirst drive you to obedience. We can wait, you know; we're well paid for what we're doing. Come, man,' Tate went on, 'don't be an idiot. You're in a corner and the sooner this is over the sooner you'll be released.'

Since there seemed to be a certain wisdom in the statement Sid did as he was told, meanwhile watching the array of scientific instruments being lined up around him. When he had finally shed every stitch of clothing the scientists took up their positions and at a signal from Tate the lights were extinguished and shutters over the windows blotted out what little deflected daylight managed to enter this built-in annexe.

There were one or two gasps, chiefly from the guards, at the vision of the glowing yellow man in the darkness: the instruments whirred and camera devices clicked. Sid felt peculiar instruments prod at him now and again and there were the sounds of the scientists talking amongst themselves. Then finally the lights came up again and Sid blinked a little.

'All right, you can dress,' Tate said briefly, glancing up from studying a panel of meters.

Sid did so. He had just reached the point of putting on his tie again when Tate said. 'When you're dressed get on that table there. We haven't finished.'

The 'table' was a sinister-looking device complete with straps and a headrest. Once again because he had no alternative, Sid did as he was told. Almost before he realized it he had been strapped immovably into position, one arm left free which was quickly clamped around the wrist by a curious instrument on rubber wheels. The whole business reminded him of some elaborate blood transfusion.

'Now,' Tate said, coming forward. 'We come to the acid test, Mr. Cassell. Whether it will hurt you or not I cannot say quite since there has never been a parallel case before. We are quite satisfied from our tests that you have indeed produced cold light within yourself by reflecting cosmic radiation instead of absorbing it. Or maybe you now that much already?'

'I know,' Sid replied. 'And a good deal more.'

'The condition is produced,' Tate continued, 'by a particular vibratory rate of the molecules composing your body, a vibratory rate never before achieved in an organic being. It has only happened now because of the hundred-thousand-volt shock you got recently. What we propose to do is determine the exact rate of that vibration, and since the process is entirely electrical you are bound to feel a good deal of — er — shall I say electrical stimulus. Hence the straps, so you cannot move at the most vital moment. You should feel quite honored. Probably you are about to give to science the secret of cold light. If the vibratory speed of molecules can be applied also to inorganic bodies, then indeed we enter a new era. Now, if you are ready?'

'It should be obvious that the pleasure's all yours,' Sid retorted.

Tate gave a wintry smile and switched on the apparatus, which was imprisoning Sid's right wrist. Immediately he gave a gasp and twisted in anguish as violent pins-and-needles writhed through his arm. He saw now that the straps were indeed serving their purpose. Violently though the current affected him there was nothing he could do to evade it — except sweat, and gasp, and writhe again.

For nearly fifteen minutes Tate kept patiently at his task, the other scientists grouped around him as they watched the reacting meters. There was plainly no thought in their minds for the torture imposed on their victim. He was simply a specimen to be analyzed.

It was when he felt that another twitch would blast the senses out of him that Sid found the power switched off. Weak and gasping he lay flat, perspiration pouring from his face. Then Tate came forward and dispassionately unfastened the straps. He handed over a colored drink.

'This will fix you,' he said briefly. 'Drink it.'

Sid raised it to his lips with a shaking hand, then he put it down again.

'No thanks. I wouldn't put it past a bunch like you to give me poison. I'll get right without it.'

Tate shrugged. 'More fool you.' He turned to a bell push and depressed it, and by the time Sid had struggled from the table and somewhat recovered himself Denham Roberts had come into the laboratory, his florid face full of eager enquiry.

'Well, gentlemen, how did it go?' he demanded.

'Excellently,' Tate replied. 'There is no mistake, Mr. Roberts. Our young friend genuinely radiates cold light, and we have been successful in trapping the wavelength — rather to his discomfiture, I'm afraid.'

'All in the cause of science,' Roberts grinned. 'You appreciate that, Cassell, of course?'

Sid gave a malignant glance. 'You needn't think the beating you've had me take is going to go unanswered, Mr. Roberts! I'll get my own back one day, on you, and Grimsby Tate here. Yes, on the whole damned bunch of you! You see if I don't!'

'It so happens,' Roberts said, 'that we do not intend to wait for that exciting moment. You surely do not suppose I intend to allow you to go free in the world to recount what has happened here, do you? No, my young friend. Not only could you make things difficult concerning the way you have been treated, but you could also inform rivals that you have cold light. That would greatly jeopardize our intended monopoly . . . I take it cold light can be commercialized, Tate?'

'Little doubt of it, sir, but I'd rather discuss it with you privately.'

'Sensible man.' Roberts nodded to the strong-arm men hovering in the background. 'On your way, boys, and take our human glow-worm with you.'

At that all Sid's fury and resentment spilled over and he lashed out violently. His very blazing anger gained him a brief ascendancy, but against so many men he was finally beaten. A blow over the head dazed him and, when he started to come to again, he realized he was bound hand and foot and lying on the floor of a shooting brake. Seated above him were his four implacable captors.

'Sorry,' apologized the spokesman, just as he had once before. 'We've got our orders, Mr. Cassell.'

'And — and what are they — ?' Sid asked wearily, giving his aching head a shake.

'Apparently you know too much, so you'll have to be disposed of. A copper mine, no longer in use, has been chosen. Everything is primed for an accident — so called. You could easily have fallen into it. At any rate that will be the story.'

Sid did not say any more. He was beyond it. And the brake kept on traveling, for perhaps a hundred miles out of London. Late in the afternoon the disused copper mine workings were reached — a deserted region in a locality that Sid could not place. He was hauled out of the brake, still bound, and carried by his four powerful captors to the mouth of an ancient shaft. Here he was set down.

The spokesman grinned briefly. 'Sorry,' he apologized, and pushed out the flat of his hand straight into Sid's face. In consequence, bound as he was, he lost his balance and toppled over the brink.

From deep down came a squelching thud, then silence. The four men looked at each other.

'Orders obeyed,' the spokesman commented, lighting a cigarette. 'Let's get back.'

3

Cold light

In his private offices, Denham Roberts held an early consultation with Grimsby Tate. The other scientists were not present since they had merely been summoned to check Tate's findings. He alone was in sole charge of the experiment.

'Using the wavelength generated by Cassell we can definitely produce cold light,' Tate said, referring to his technical notes. 'It is accomplished by a rearrangement of the molecules which causes them to transmit cosmic radiation instead of absorbing it. The result of that is pretty much the same as a mirror reflecting a beam of sunlight.'

'Yes, yes, but I am not a scientist, Tate,' Roberts broke in impatiently. 'Tell me in plain language what we have to do and how much it is going to cost.'

'What you have to do is subject some material — preferably copper since it has high conductivity — to this wavelength for a given period, which I haven't worked out exactly, and there you have it.'

'Have it?' Roberts looked vague. 'You don't mean that is *all* we do?'

'Certainly.' Tate was patient because he was being well paid. 'What happens is this: first, from a projector, we produce the wavelength which exactly duplicates that being emanated by Cassell.'

'But *how* do we duplicate it, and what would we use?'

'Electricity, and transformers specially wired so that the current is altered to the particular wavelength we want. It is purely a contortion of the principle of radio and television. Any wavelength can be produced by an exact transformer winding. But to know its exact wavelength one has to know of its existence first, if you understand me, which is why we tested young Cassell. The very production of cold light produces a wavelength and that, basically, must be the same as the original exciting cause.'

'Oh — I see.' Roberts breathed heavily and bit the end from a cigar. He did not look as though he saw in the slightest.

'Therefore the cost to you will be that of a transformer and projector — and afterwards the negligible cost of infusing copper blocks, shaped like lamps if you wish, which once impregnated with this wavelength, will give off cold light for ever, or at least for as long as cosmic rays exist. And when they cease,' Tate finished dryly, 'you and I will hardly be in a position to worry.'

'I still don't get it,' Roberts declared flatly. 'Don't these copper blocks want recharging regularly, or something? What the devil keeps them alight?'

'Cosmic radiation.'

'But *how*?'

Tate meditated for a moment. 'Look, Mr. Roberts, let us take a simple example. Suppose you have an ordinary mirror covered with a cloth, a black one for preference. Now, you put the mirror in the sunlight, still covered: What happens? The black cloth absorbs the sunlight but does not reflect it. Right?'

'Even I can grasp that,' the big man said heavily.

'Assume now that this mirror is a copper block. It too, in the normal way, absorbs cosmic radiation, or sunlight to hold to our simile. Now, you project a given wavelength at the copper and immediately its molecular make-up undergoes a change, so that it no longer absorbs radiation; it reflects it. This is equivalent to you stripping the black cloth from your mirror, and what do you get? A reflected beam of sunlight. Does that mirror ever need re-charging as long as the sun shines? No. In the same way the copper block never will need it as long as cosmic rays exist. And they pour down night and day and pass through everything except dense lead. So the lamps are eternal. What Cassell discovered, albeit accidentally, is a wavelength which changes the atomic make-up of any organic or inorganic object so as to make it reflect cosmic radiation instead of absorb it. Anything in the world can therefore be made luminous.'

'We don't want that, though,' Roberts said, thinking. 'It would be too wholesale. Our objective must be lamps to start with. Your suggestion of copper fashioned in the form of a lamp is a good one. I assume we can only get light, not power?'

'Not power, no. That will still be generated as now. But light is at your command, possible anywhere except perhaps in deep mines or in heavily insulated vaults. For all practical purposes the cold light lamp will work anywhere.'

'At a cost of a projector and special transformer?'

'Exactly.'

Roberts rubbed his hands. 'Get to work on the financial details, Tate, and I can put it before my colleagues. Whether they say yes or no doesn't signify in the slightest since I shall go ahead in any case. For the sake of form, though, they must be consulted. That doesn't mean they will know the secret wavelength or how to produce cold light. That belongs to us exclusively, of course.'

'Of course.' Tate smiled thinly. 'Fifty-fifty.'

Roberts snatched his cigar out of his mouth. 'Eh?'

'I said fifty-fifty. I'm scientist enough to know that this cold light idea will sweep the world once it is launched. I am the only one who can work out the necessary formula — but without your financial aid and connections it would be no use to me. And no other influential body would listen to me due to my being discredited recently in the press. But together we are an ideal combination. Naturally I cannot think of working for anything less than half, and I will have my own auditor keep a check on receipts. It's that, or nothing.'

'Very well,' Roberts growled round his cigar. 'Fifty-fifty it is.'

'I expect to have this formula worked out late tonight,' the scientist added. 'Also the design of a projector, transformer, and so forth, together with estimate of cost. I will hand it all over to you in return for your contract, agreeing to our fifty-fifty basis and an advance royalty check of one hundred thousand pounds.'

'Advance royalty on something that has never been marketed! Do you take me for a darned fool, man?'

'I take you for a business man. You have got to have that formula, therefore you must be prepared to pay for it.'

Roberts mused. 'Here is a better plan, from my point of view. Retain the formula — don't even let me see it, but make a model lamp for me to see. Call on me for the expenses for projector and so forth and let me see the goods in the window. If I like what I see you shall have your check, and you will hand over the formula.'

'Done,' the scientist agreed, and they shook hands on it. Then Roberts sat back in his chair and meditated.

'Now to what we might call the side issues. What about those other scientists who worked with you? How much do they know? How much harm can they do us? In a project as big as this may prove I wouldn't trust one of 'em.'

Tate smiled composedly. 'You can be sure I have safeguarded everything. Those gentlemen only checked my figures and helped with the experiment upon Cassell. They cannot possibly know the vital wavelength, which is the secret because I kept charge of the instrument that revealed it. The figures they checked were merely subsidiary and not the main issue.'

'Then they can be paid for their trouble and dropped forthwith?'

'No reason why not. What I am wondering is what did you do with Cassell?'

'Nothing,' Roberts grinned. 'That is, I wouldn't be such a fool as to stick my chin out like that, but my men have, I hope, followed out orders and disposed of him. A well-contrived 'accident', if you understand, always granting he can ever be found. That I very much doubt.'

'You mean you've had him killed?'

'By now he should be dead, yes. An accident that can never be traced back to me.'

Tate sat back in his chair, his eyes thoughtful. Roberts looked at him in surprise.

'Dammit, man, I couldn't leave him lying around after what we did to him, could I?'

'Certainly not. I'm only hoping you

haven't been too premature.'

'Meaning what?'

'Meaning that if he is dead — as presumably he is by now — his secret will literally have died with him. His death will destroy the molecular peculiarity that produces cold light. If there is any mistake in my figuring I shall never have a second chance.'

Roberts threw his cigar in the ashtray. 'I thought you said you had everything worked out! Why all that damned palaver with Cassell if you're not sure?'

'I *am* sure, as near as it is humanly possible to be, but there is always the unknown factor. I would have felt happier had he just been held captive until I'd had time to experiment. I hadn't realized you intended to kill him. My mind was much occupied at the time.'

Roberts compressed his lips and hesitated over saying something; then the nearer telephone rang. He picked it up.

'Roberts speaking. Yes?' He listened in silence to a few brief words. 'All right. Thanks.'

He put the 'phone down again and

looked at the scientist. 'There is our answer, Tate. That was Drew, my right-hand man. He only said, 'Job done as ordered,' but that means Cassell is now at the bottom of a two hundred foot deep mining shaft, probably deep down under the mud. In other words — finished!'

Tate got to his feet. 'In that case I'll push on with the formula and satisfy myself that all is well. See you later, Mr. Roberts, when I've something worthwhile to report.'

With that the scientist took his departure and Roberts was left scowling with uncertainty. The thought that he had perhaps killed the goose that laid the golden eggs before being sure it could lay at all was a horrifying one.

Had he known of certain facts, however, he need not have worried — or, perhaps, he would have worried a great deal more, depending upon the condition of his conscience. For Sidney Cassell was not dead, though he was certainly savagely knocked about. He was, about the time Roberts had received his 'phone call, lying in the very shallow mud at the base of the mineshaft. He was in total darkness, bruised from head to foot, and from the feel of things had one arm broken. What had saved him from death had been the mud itself. It had acted as a shock absorber, cushioning his fall. So, though he was severely jolted and his head ached fit to burst he was still alive, in pain, and squirming in the mud as best he could to get himself clear of it.

It was his writhing movements that brought him abruptly against something rough and metallic. It was his bound hands that encountered it first — so he maneuvered into a position whereby he could more easily feel what the object was. In time he decided it was a broken piece of iron prop, evidently from the time when the shaft had been in working order. It had jagged edges, and that was the very thing he required.

At the end of fifteen minutes, for his movements were slow with his injured arm, he felt the tight cords about his wrists give way as they frayed through. Another five minutes released his ankles, then in the pitchy darkness he stood up, his feet slopping around in the mud.

He began to move, breathing hard and wincing with every step. After a while he realized that he had become free of the mud and was walking along what was probably one of the old mine tunnels. He tested every step he took, in case he plunged to fresh destruction, his sound hand and arm guiding him along the wall. Every movement he made was anguish, for both his head and his arm, but he kept on going. He *had* to. There must be a way out of the maze somehow. Then, presently, as the caked mud began to fall from him an eerie glow came forth, primrose yellow, and lighting the way clearly enough to his dark-accustomed eyes.

He smiled rather bitterly to himself at the realization that he had become his own flashlamp! Evidently even down here cosmic radiation was reaching, unhampered by rocks, and there was not enough lead content to form a blockage.

So, following tunnel after tunnel, always with sufficient light to see his way, and always going upwards, he came at last to a clear draught of fresh air. It led inevitably to the open and he ultimately clawed his way out through a maze of ancient timbers. Exhausted, he lay down in the coppery-red dust around the opening and looked about him.

There was nothing in sight except the old mine workings and abandoned pyramids of debris from excavations. Not a person in sight and the stillness of the late afternoon sunlight.

Sid thought of many things as he lay there trying to recover. He thought of the treachery of Mary, the ruthlessness of Denham Roberts, the cold scientific probing of Grimsby Tate — and the casual push in the face that had toppled him into the shaft. But at the end of it all he was not dead, and nobody knew of it yet except himself. In that fact there perhaps lay power — the power to avenge.

And now? Well, obviously he had to get his arm put right and have an examination. From the feel of things there were more things than just his arm broken. He had to find the nearest doctor. If he could reach that doctor without anybody else seeing him, the doctor certainly would not betray anything about his patient.

Wait until nightfall; nothing else for it. Sid gritted his teeth at the thought, but because his desire for revenge was greater than the suffering he was enduring he resolved to stay where he was until dark. Nobody was likely to come here.

Nor did they. Hour after hour he remained, aching in every limb, longing for a drink, his exposed skin covered now with a fine reddish dust, the residue of copper which lay everywhere around this abandoned place. Then at last, as sunset approached, he fought his way to his feet, staggered a little, and braced himself for an effort. When he began walking he felt a little steadier, though his head and arm still ached unendurably.

He looked a fantastic figure as he made his way out of the mine workings to a rough road nearby. His clothes were plastered in red mud and his face and hands were deep red with the dried dust. He preferred it that way. It would to some extent mitigate the glow he would emanate when darkness really fell. The thing to do was find a doctor by twilight before he really became luminescent; then in the bright lights of the doctor's surgery nothing untoward would be visible.

The fortune that had so far been eluding him this time came to his rescue. In half an hour, as the real darkness was settling, he came to a village not far from the old mine. In the single main street between the cottages one or two children ceased their play to stare at the ragged, mud-caked stranger. Two of them ran home, plainly scared out of their wits. Sid looked at those who remained and came to a stop.

'Where do I find a doctor around here?' he asked.

A little boy answered him. 'End of the street, mister. You can see his board hanging out there.'

Sid looked, nodded, and shambled on his way. He was glad he had been directed by children. They have notoriously short memories and would soon forget all about him. The trouble now would come if the doctor were not at home, though he ought to be at this hour of the evening.

He was — a pink-faced, elderly practitioner who looked at his visitor curiously as he entered the surgery. The luck was still holding since the doctor himself had opened the door. No maid, nobody who might talk. Possibly this village medico did not even possess a maid, or else it was her night off.

'Fallen down the old mine workings, of course?' the doctor asked, and Sid gave him a sharp look.

'I didn't say so.'

'You don't have to. I recognize the copper dust. If it's any consolation to you you're not the first who's taken a dive in that mine, by any means. Anyway, what's the trouble?'

'Arm and head are killing me. Give me a look-over, will you?'

The doctor nodded and went to work. Sid remained silent, wincing now and again. It was half an hour later when the doctor was finished and Sid had his arm in splints and a rough sling round his neck. The dirt and mud had been removed from his face and hands. On the back of his head was a large plaster.

'Fractured arm, certainly,' the doctor said, 'but it's not a serious one. Your head's okay except for a deep cut. You'll get over the ache after a sleep. In fact you're a lucky man.'

Sid smiled sardonically. 'That's a matter of opinion, Doc. Well, I'm not a regular patient of yours so how much do I owe you?'

The doctor named a surprisingly small sum then looked at him curiously. 'Where do you hail from, young man?'

'It doesn't matter,' Sid answered curtly, handing over a mud-caked note. 'I just don't want my visit here to be talked about. Understand?'

'Naturally I shall respect your confidence, as I would that of any patient. The only case where I might fail to do so would be if the police were to question me.'

'Police?' Sid looked surprised, then smiled gravely. 'Oh, you needn't worry. I'm not a criminal. Tell me, how long will this arm of mine take to get right?'

'That depends. I'd like you to call and see me each day for a while.'

Sid was silent. He was in a village where probably nothing had happened or ever would. He was out of sight of the world. At the moment, with his arm like this, he was in no position to wander very far. He made up his mind swiftly.

'I'm a stranger in these parts, doctor, but I could stay here for a few days as well as anywhere else. Can you recommend anybody who would take me in? At least until my arm is better?'

The doctor smiled. 'You don't have to move any further, young man. My wife and I would be glad to put you up — for a trifling consideration, of course. There is a spare room you can have.'

'That's very kind of you. Here's my money, by the way. When it's dried out it should be as good as new.'

Sid put several notes on the table and added a little heap of coins. The doctor looked at it and then nodded.

'Come and meet my wife, Mr. — er — '

'The name is Desmond Smith,' Sid improvised.

'Ah, yes. This way, Mr. Smith, and I'll

also see what I can do towards lending you some clothes. We're pretty much of a size, I think.'

* * *

Whilst Sid Cassell made a thorough job of keeping himself out of sight in a remote West Country village, Grimsby Tate, the physicist, completed his complicated experiments with cold light.

Nobody made any inquiries about Sid Cassell. Mary Carter, the only one who, in the normal way, might have made inquiry had taken herself off to France on holiday with the money that Denham Roberts had given her for her 'work.' Sid had no particular friends who were interested enough to find out what had become of him, and his apartment rent was paid up in advance so there were no inquiries from that end, either. Indeed only one person did wonder, and that was Dr. Craymond. For the life of him he could not understand why Sid had not kept his appointment, and because cold light was at stake the scientist began to think, after some days, that maybe he ought to inquire into matters.

Then, four days after he had last seen Roberts, Grimsby Tate reappeared in the big man's office carrying a small specimen box. He placed it on the broad desk and motioned to it.

'There it is,' he announced, as matter-of-fact as ever. 'Fortunately for us my calculations were correct, so we do not need Cassell again, even if we could have him. Cold light is an established fact. I think you said you wished to see if you — liked it?'

'Certainly!' Roberts looked eagerly at the box. 'When do we start?'

'If your laboratory is at liberty we can start now. And for obvious reasons we do not wish anybody else present except ourselves.'

'That's all there will be. Nobody in there at the moment. Come along.'

Roberts led the way quickly from his office, as eager as a schoolboy about to attack a forbidden hamper of tuck. Tate was as casual as ever as he followed into the laboratory, closing the door behind him. Then he closed the shutters over the windows, but left the normal lights on. This fact made Roberts frown.

'Don't we want those off, too?'

'No. I want you to compare this cold-light lamp with the normal two-hundred watt lamps we have in here. There are six of them, observe. They look to be emanating pure white light — but watch what happens when we have light as it really should be.'

Roberts watched, motionless. The scientist's hands unclamped the specimen box. Immediately from the depths of the box there fanned a pearly luster of snow-white brilliance. Smiling gravely, like a magician performing a superb trick, Tate reached into the box and brought forth something that blazed light in every direction. His hands looked as though they were bathed in some uncanny spiritual fire as he raised aloft a pear-shaped object, dimly visible as a darker nucleus amidst the literal blaze of glory.

Yet that light, for all its tremendous intensity and steady brilliance, did not hurt the eye. It penetrated into the darkest corners; it made the normal lamps look dirty yellow by comparison. It revealed flaws in the otherwise spotless laboratory walls.

'Cold light!' Tate exclaimed, emotional for a brief moment. 'Light such as we have never known before. Sunlight itself, the radiation of space, and cool as a mountain spring. Here — feel for yourself.'

Roberts hesitated for a moment and then took the flaming white pear in his hands. Not a suggestion of warmth touched him. Fascinated, he stared at the pulse-free flow of pearly radiance gushing up from between his fingers.

'Ten of these could light a city!' he cried exultantly.

'Easily,' Tate acknowledged, 'or else a few giant ones. There is no limit to the size. That object is intended to light a building the size of a powerhouse. It is only shaped copper, impregnated, so that its molecular order is changed. With it, Mr. Roberts, cold light becomes an established fact!'

Roberts looked again into the glare and then set the pear down on the bench. Tate moved towards him.

'Well, sir, do you like what you see?'

'Need you ask that? What about the formula? You have it with you?'

'I have. I thought we might complete our initial arrangement.'

'Come to my office,' Roberts said promptly.

Tate gave a quiet nod, picked up the cold lamp and put it back in the box, then followed after the big man down the corridor. In fifteen minutes the preliminaries were completed and Tate had his check in lieu of advance royalties, and the necessary contract guaranteeing a fifty-fifty return on profits.

'Which makes everything satisfactory,' Roberts said lighting a cigar. 'You and I will handle this business between us, Tate. No other parties. Just Roberts and Tate, Cold Light Engineers. I'll go to work immediately on the advance publicity. I'll handle the business side and you stick to the scientific end. I suppose you have a copy of the formula you've given me?'

Tate gave his thin smile. 'In the bank

on micro-film. I'm not a man who takes chances.'

'No — of course not.' Roberts gave him a steady look that might have implied almost anything; then he got to his feet. 'Better let me handle things for the moment, Tate, and I'll tell you when there is anything definite.'

And with that Tate departed. Roberts reached to the phone and spoke over the private wire.

'Drew? D.R. speaking. Tate is just leaving the building with my check and a contract. You know exactly what to do.'

'Very good, Mr. Roberts.' And the line became dead.

Roberts smiled to himself and again took the cold light lamp out of the box and stared at it. The office was filled with unholy white fire. He wondered, as he returned the lamp to its resting place, why he did not afterwards find himself gazing at everything through a sea of flame, due to reaction on the retinas. That he did not lay in the very nature of the cold light. As ordinary daylight leaves no dazzle persistence of vision in the eye, so this outpouring of reflected cosmic radiation did not affect the optic nerves either. It was light of unimaginable beauty, delicacy, and overwhelming brilliance. It was trapped daylight.

Being a businessman Denham Roberts mused over these things, debating also the best manufacturers to handle tens of thousands of lamps, manufacturers who could not themselves destroy his intended monopoly. The planning and organization before him was after his own heart. He would flood the world with Roberts Lamps, and he alone would reap the benefit. Such indeed was the measure of his faith in Drew, his strong-arm man.

And it was faith which was justified, for late that evening the body of Grimsby Tate was discovered by a patrolling policeman lying in an entry, nearly stripped of clothes and the head battered ruthlessly. The matter was reported to Scotland Yard but the man who worried least was Drew — past master in the art of murder, he knew he would never be detected, or the man who had helped him.

Which left Denham Roberts as the controller of the cold-light secret. Or so he imagined. He could hardly know that Dr. Craymond, of the Electro-Physical Laboratory, puzzled by the continued silence of Sidney Cassell — and absence from his apartment — had seen fit to visit Scotland Yard and give them the facts. This happened two days after the murder of Grimsby Tate and to Chief Inspector Hodge in charge of the Tate mystery, Craymond's visit was of especial interest.

'And this man Cassell should have reported to you for a physical examination?' Hodge asked thoughtfully.

Craymond nodded. 'Purely for the purposes of scientific research. I had reason to think that Mr. Cassell possessed the secret of cold light — a physical condition produced by a violent electric shock he had recently received. Since cold light is purely a matter of scientific interest I will not go into that — but I will say that Mr. Cassell mentioned enemies or at least a concern anxious to get his secret from him. He told me the Power and Light Combine were after him, and he had just had a brush with its president.'

'Then?' Hodge asked.

'He wanted to come right away to see me and would have done so, only some curious appointment stopped him. I haven't seen or heard from him since.'

'All very interesting,' Hodge mused. 'Two days ago a scientist by the name of Grimsby Tate was found murdered. Tate's record was not a savory one, but that does not concern us particularly. The interesting part is that he worked for the president of the Power and Light Combine. We found out that much, though we can't prove who killed him.'

'Tate?' Craymond repeated. 'I didn't know about his death since I seldom read the newspapers or watch the News. I do know though that he was mixed up in some international scandal — and I also know he was one of the best physicists in the country. In fact just the man to analyze cold light.'

'Meaning?' Hodge asked, seeing the faraway look in Craymond's eyes.

'I'm not quite sure. Just a thought.

Cassell has vanished. Tate was murdered, and we know Denham Roberts wanted Cassell's secret. Only a scientist like Tate could have discovered it. What does it suggest to you?'

'I'm too wary an old bird to say,' Hodge smiled, 'but thanks for the suggestion. I'll go to work on it . . . '

And he did so — but, though every line of normal investigation pointed directly to the guilt of Denham Roberts, particularly when the hoardings, newspapers and television started advertising his marvelous cold light lamps, there was just no way of proving what he had done. And without proof Hodge was hamstrung.

So Roberts got away with it, exactly as he had planned he would, and gradually his immense publicity campaign, backed entirely by his own finances and having nothing to do with the Power and Light Combine, began to have an effect. When, a couple of months after the death of Tate, he was ready to market his first cold-light lamps — now patented in his name — there was not a man, woman, or child in the country who did not know what they could do. The demonstration he had arranged in one of London's largest Exhibition halls clinched the matter completely. Thereafter Roberts had little to do but manufacture and sell and watch his bank balance grow.

* * *

In a certain West Country village Sid Cassell was fully aware of what was happening and had arrived at the conclusion it was time he emerged from seclusion and did something to regain the miracle that he had endured so much to produce. So, sound again now in wind and limb and having been adequately cared for in the interval by the kindly doctor and his wife, he decided one morning upon departure.

'Don't mind my saying it,' the doctor remarked, as he saw Sid to the door, 'but I think this business of cold-light lamps has a lot to do with you.'

'Oh?' Sid endeavored to look casual. 'What makes you think that?'

'I happen to have noticed you once or

twice after dark, even though you have tried to keep to your room. The first time I had a shock; the second time I started thinking. Then I put two and two together.'

'Meaning?'

'You should read the newspapers. A man answering your description is missing and the police are trying to discover what has happened to him. A Dr. Craymond has said that in the dark this missing man glows brightly due to some electrical phenomenon or other.' The doctor gave a direct look. 'You are Sidney Cassell, aren't you?'

Sid knew it was no use keeping up the pretence any longer.

'Yes. I am. But I don't want the fact broadcast. I greatly appreciate all that you have done for me but — well, to be exact, my secret was stolen from me and enemies tried to kill me. At the moment they believe me dead. I want them to go on thinking that; it will make it simpler for me.'

'I understand, Mr. Cassell, and you may rely on me implicitly. I'll never give you away.' The doctor hesitated. 'There is one point, though, which I think you should know about.'

'Yes?' Sid picked up his bag and waited again.

'I'm afraid that you are no longer unique. I have the same 'defect' as you.'

4

Contagion

There was a momentary silence whilst Sid absorbed the doctor's astounding statement. Apparently it was not a joke. He was too mature and experienced a man to indulge in facetiousness in a matter so important.

'Same power as me?' Sid asked. 'But you can't have! It's impossible!'

'Then come into the surgery and tell me what you think. I have had no night calls, fortunately, but when I do I'll have to get a locum to deal with them.'

Wondering, Sid followed the doctor across the hall. In the surgery the blinds were drawn, and immediately the doctor became visible, his face and hands a primrose yellow. Sid himself was by this time a bluish-purple, on his way to the composite of all wavelengths — pure white.

Not that Sid was interested in himself at the moment: it was the astounding vision of the doctor that held him. Definitely he had got the cold light complex but not yet very advanced.

'Well,' came the medico's voice. 'Satisfied?'

'More than,' Sid muttered, and stood frowning as the daylight was restored. 'I just don't understand it.'

'Neither do I. I've been reading in the papers about this cold light business — as much as the scientists will reveal, or can reveal, that is — And as far as I can see it can't possibly be contagious. Yet I've got it.'

Sid could only nod, too baffled to make a comment. The doctor was obviously not afraid of his condition. His manner was more one of utter mystification.

'No suggestions?' he asked at last.

'None. I'm not a scientist, Doc — only an electrical maintenance engineer, but I feel I owe it to you to find out what caused you to become like me. There's a physicist I can contact for an explanation. When I get it I'll let you know.'

‘Good enough for me,’ the doctor smiled, and for the second time he saw Sid to the door.

This time Sid really did get started on his journey, and he considered the slight disguise he wore sufficient for his purposes. Dark glasses, a soft hat pulled well down — whereas he had never worn a hat before — and a small moustache that he had grown in the intervening time since his ‘death.’ He felt safe enough, particularly as nobody would be looking for him — and the country doctor he trusted implicitly.

But how in the name of the devil had he, too, become a victim of cold light radiation? It was utterly beyond Sid’s understanding. He pondered it all the way in the train to London and was still no nearer when he landed in the capital.

Here he almost immediately found the advertisements for Roberts Cold Light Lamps shouting at him from every side. There was nowhere he could look but he saw them — and not only the advertisements but the lamps themselves.

They were in many parts of the terminus and for quite a while he gazed in wonder at the curious pear-shaped object which shed daylight without shadows over a seemingly limitless area.

Then he went on again, booked himself in at an obscure hotel in the city center and here reviewed the position in which he found himself. The first necessity was to find a position of some kind, for his spare cash had run out — as indeed it would have done long before had not the country doctor been so moderate in his demands. What money he had in the bank he could not touch if he wished to preserve his identity and confirm the belief that he was dead.

To find a position would not be easy, unless somebody with influence could help him. It was thus that his thoughts turned to Dr. Craymond, about the only person likely to understand his predicament. So he rang up the Physical Laboratory and, by hints without direct statement, explained who he was and made an appointment to see the scientist in his hotel that same evening.

Craymond arrived, a very puzzled man, and it took him a few moments to confirm his belief that Sid was Sid when he first saw him. The removal of the dark glasses finally convinced him. Being in the privacy of his own room Sid promptly relapsed into his normal manner and tossed the glasses to one side.

'Dr. Craymond, I'm in one hell of a pickle,' he explained frankly.

'So I gather.' The physicist frowned. 'Are you not aware that the police are trying to find you, to tie you up with the death of Grimsby Tate? He was murdered, you know, shortly after your disappearance.'

'He was? That's a disappointment. I was going to take care of him myself. However, let me tell you what's been happening to me — and I'm relying on you not to tell a soul what I'm going to tell you. If ever a man had a reason for wanting to get his own back, I have.'

'Carry on,' the physicist invited, and listened without interrupting as Sid gave all the details. He did not hold back anything for he had the instinctive feeling that the physicist would respect his confidence. 'So you see, Roberts got me after all,' Sid finished. 'Now I'm on my last few pounds and looking for a job. When I get one I shall systematically go to work to reclaim the formula which Roberts and Tate between them stole from me.'

'Quite understandable — but what is this about a country doctor having the same peculiarity as yourself?'

Sid got up and began to move restlessly. 'That's what I want to find out about. No doubt that he has it, Dr. Craymond, only he's only at the red stage of luminescence whereas I'm nearly bluish purple.'

'But it's impossible!' Craymond insisted. 'Utterly impossible. This cold light effect isn't something which one person can hand to another either wittingly or unwittingly. He must be mistaken, or else for some reason of his own the doctor is playing a trick.'

'He isn't that type. And why should he want to, anyway? He's a sober, responsible man of sixty-odd. I told him I'd try and find the solution — but I gather you haven't one?'

'Not off-hand, I haven't. Maybe if I saw and examined the doctor for myself I might find something.'

Sid reflected over this, then Craymond added urgently: 'In fact I think I should see him. He'll be just as useful as a scientific specimen as you will. In spite of Roberts launching his cold lamps, science is still as anxious to have the cold light secret for itself — and that offer I made you still goes. Or rather I shall have to amend it if the doctor comes into it. If both of you are useful the amount payable will have to be split between you.'

Sid's expression changed. 'Nothing doing! I'm the original cold-light man and whatever rewards there are I refuse to share with anybody else. Forget all about what I said. The doc will have to work out his puzzle for himself.'

'It's most unlikely he will ever do that, which leaves him around for other scientific bodies to examine — those in other countries for example. We want the secret entirely to ourselves because it's not the kind of thing it is safe to share.'

'And to what use can science put this cold light secret?' Sid demanded. 'Roberts has already got started, and it's more than a certainty that he'll have patented his discovery. We can't do anything about that — not without the proof that he stole the secret from me.'

'You can safely leave the details to the Electro-Physical Laboratory,' Craymond answered. 'I know the facts, and I believe them. We will find a way to put Roberts out of business — but before I can do anything you must submit to our examination and so must this doctor.'

'And money still halved?'

'It will have to be. Sir Devenish Rondel, head of the Lab, is by no means sanguine of your possibilities even as it is.'

Sid pondered through an interval, then turned back to where the physicist sat waiting for him to speak.

'I've just been thinking, Dr. Craymond. As I told you when I was thrown into that mine by Roberts's strong-arm man I got myself smothered in copper deposits and copper dust. I was still in that condition when I first contacted my friend the doctor. Do you suppose that could in any way have accounted for my transmitting my 'peculiarity' to him?'

Craymond did not answer immediately. In fact it took him several minutes to weigh things up, and he finished with an expression of profound surprise.

'I believe it might be possible, yes. The effect is basically electrical, and copper transmits an electrical emanation more easily than most substances. Yes, it's a possibility! The curious molecular change you have undergone, and the emanation from it could have been conducted to the doctor by copper contact. I could find out for sure if you asked him to have an examination.'

Sid shook his head, his jaw set stubbornly. 'No, I shall not do that. Nor shall I submit to an examination on my own account. I went through enough hell when Tate experimented and I'm scared of any more. There are too many damned wolves barking at my door to get my secret and I've no guarantee but what I'll be left high and dry in the rush, as I have been in the case of Roberts.'

'You surely don't doubt but that the Electro-Physical Laboratory will honor its obligations in the matter of payment?'

'I don't doubt that for a moment. On the other hand I do not like the premature misgivings of Sir Devenish Rondel, nor the idea of the amount being halved with the doctor. If I do not submit to experiment I have no need to ask him to do so either. Finally, nothing would prevent the Electro-Physical Laboratory from publicizing the story of cold light far and wide and that would reveal that I am alive and kicking.'

'Well?'

'I prefer to be thought dead.'

'But why? Roberts will be dealt with by us — '

'Maybe and maybe not. He'll be so legally tied up it may take more than the best brains in the Electro-Physical Laboratory's legal department to get the better of him. If I work out my own plan I'll smash Roberts completely, without legal help.'

'Which means you do not intend to

submit to experiment?' Craymond rose to his feet.

'Right! At least not yet. Do me the favor of keeping it quiet that I am alive and when I am good and ready I'll hand myself over. If you say anything about my being still in the land of the living you won't get a thing out of me, the agents of Roberts will see to that. Understand?'

Craymond sighed. 'Up to you. I cannot force you, of course. But what about money? You said you need a job. How will you go about getting one?'

'I'll think of something. I only want enough to live on: the rest of my time I shall devote to those various people who encompassed my downfall. Roberts, that strong-arm thug of his, and Mary Carter, the girl I trusted.' Sid clenched his fist. 'I'll deal with each of them, and when I have I'll come to you, not until.'

'And this doctor in the West country?'

'He must take his chance.'

With Sid's mind obviously so set on vengeance there was nothing more the physicist could do, so he took his departure. Sid for his part went down into the hotel lounge, secured an early edition of the evening paper, and thereafter began a systematic scouring of the 'Situations Vacant' column. All he wanted for the moment was enough to live on — some kind of job that would only make demands upon him by day, then at night he could retreat from sight. Certainly he would have to depart from the hotel and find a room somewhere cheap, still under the name of Desmond Smith. His plan, apart from the scheme of vengeance, which he had yet to develop, involved other factors. The statement of Craymond that probably the copper dust had passed on the 'complaint' to the country doctor was something that obsessed his mind. If it had been passed on in one case — why not another?

So Sid began to work out his own destiny and, in the heart of the city, Denham Roberts tackled the endless string of orders which kept coming in to him for cold lamps of all shapes and sizes. By this time he had devised all manner of designs for the lamps — and all manner of people bought from him, or at least they sent in their orders to be dealt with in strict rotation. They included hotels by the score, highway committees, shipping lines, aircraft companies, and tens of thousands of private dwelling-house owners who considered the sum being asked for a set of four lamps was far cheaper than everlastingly paying the power combine for electric current.

Definitely the Power and Light Combine would have gone out of existence altogether had cold light been able to provide power as well. Since it could not there was still a reason for the Power and Light Combine to continue operations — but it did gradually dawn upon the directors thereof that Roberts, as President of the Combine, was cutting his own throat by also being managing director of his now immensely prosperous cold light concern.

A board meeting was called and Roberts was given two alternatives, either to cut in the Power Combine for a share of the profits in cold light, or else resign. Roberts promptly resigned. He had quite enough to do in any case, his own headquarters now occupying an enormous white stone building in the center of the city, his own name blazoned in cold light lamps at the summit of the edifice . . . Yes, things were going very nicely for Denham Roberts. All the world was coming to his door and all over the world the night was becoming brighter than the day.

One particularly interested in the developments was a truck driver in the East End. He called himself Desmond Smith and seemed a moody, unsociable individual who never mixed with others more than his work demanded. Promptly at five when his work was finished, he departed for a room he occupied near the dock area. In a word, Sid had found his job. It kept him going and, meanwhile, he watched what happened in the West Country. He had a standing order for the newspapers that covered West Country activities and in a scrapbook he had columns of curious facts.

The most arresting column of all referred to 'Phantoms in Mervale' — Mervale being the name of the village where he had met the country doctor. According to the reporter there was a scare afoot in the village. Luminous people had been seen at night, sometimes in the streets, sometimes in the fields, and the good villagers were firmly of the opinion that the devil himself was abroad. Since it was only a village tale and had never even been reported in the national newspapers, the matter was just ignored as sheer superstition — but for Sid it spelt something very much different. His cuttings showed that four people had been seen as luminous, two of them young women, which seemed to suggest that the good doctor was now not alone in his 'glory,' but that the trouble had spread.

Sid wondered if he ought to make an occasion to go down to Mervale and look into things — then he decided against it. He had dropped out of sight and it was better he remained that way. If things worked out as he now believed they would, Mervale would finally hit the headlines. For the truth of the matter was that the cold light malady was contagious, and Sid had been the only one so far to grasp this fact. It was probable that the cold light emanation of itself was incapable of being transmitted when in its incipient stages, such as at the red end of the spectrum — but later, in the blue-white and almost final stage, it was intensely contagious. Sid himself had found this out by means of various electrical gadgets with which he was familiar from his earlier work as a maintenance engineer. This showed that he was emanating a tremendous electrical current, enough to give anybody a violent jolt if he grasped hold of them — which was one reason why he remained apparently unsociable at work and kept clear of all company.

The only analysis of the situation he could make was that, when impregnated on the surface skin with copper dust, he had definitely transmitted the molecular-changing energy to the doctor, who had then had his own molecules rearranged. He, later in his profession, had been forced to handle many people — far more than the four reported in the paper

— and they in turn had received an electric jolt because by this time his own development of the 'malady' must have reached the yellow or blue-white stage whereby it could be transmitted without the benefit of copper impregnation or anything else.

Which seemed to suggest it would be like chain reaction. One would touch another, and another and another, until —

Sid grinned as he thought of these things and decided it was time he put his own plan into action. So he devised a form of protective clothing by which he could go out at night and, like an avenging presence, he roamed the quietest streets he could find, looking for a victim.

His methods were simple. His face and left hand were covered in black rubber, his right hand was bare — a glowing member pushed in his overcoat pocket. When he passed a solitary man or woman he gripped that person momentarily by the throat and then fled on his way. The effect of this was always to stun his victim into unconsciousness for a brief while from the force of the electrical power he emanated. Accordingly no victim had a clear remembrance of him, but inevitably every man or woman he attacked found that he or she had developed all the symptoms of cold light.

By day Sid carried on with his job, feeling entirely safe from the police who were looking into the puzzle of the ghostly attacker. Chief-Inspector Hodge was on the job again, but for all the efforts of himself and his men he failed to trace the whereabouts of the unknown, the details of him being so scanty.

After six attacks Sid ceased his activities. He had done all he needed — unless he had completely misjudged the situation. But he had not. Those who had been attacked naturally came into contact with other people, and so there gradually spread into the city an increasing wave of cold light. Men, women and children everywhere were contracting the strange 'disease,' and since most of them were hardly aware how they had received it, except for the electrical jolt they had had at the moment of contact — only a slight one from those not as far developed as Sid — the memory of an original attacker was forgotten and the complaint was put down to the Roberts lamps themselves.

Which was exactly the way Sid wanted it. To various papers he wrote letters, always under different names, asking if the cold lamps were safe. Was there some strange quality in them, which was going to turn people into walking glow-worms? Had the Roberts company thoroughly and scientifically tested the lamps before putting them on the market?

Sid did not spare himself. Apart from his letters he spread the spirit of uneasiness amongst all the men and women with whom he came in contact at work, always taking care never to actually touch them. As a propaganda expert seeking to destroy the cold light prosperity that Denham Roberts had built up he was extremely proficient.

And Roberts was definitely beginning to feel the draught. Orders had dropped off by seventy-five per cent. Men and women deputations besieged his headquarters demanding an explanation for their strange and terrifying malady. Medical experts were kept busy diagnosing the more frightened ones, and in consequence the medics themselves became victims.

Still Sid waited, and watched. Matters now had reached the stage where one luminous person was no more remarkable than another. They could be seen in the streets any night — sometimes as many as half-a-dozen in a row. So that meant that he himself did not have to resort any more to protective coverings. He could go out as he wished and call himself one of the afflicted.

Thus it was that late one evening he entered the Roberts Cold Light office and walked up the broad, opulent staircase to the top floor where Denham Roberts had his office. Sid knew he would be there: he had kept careful tabs on the big man's movements for many weeks past.

He knocked lightly on the door, was told irritably to enter, and did so. He closed the door behind him and stood, a weird figure with his snow-white gleaming face and hands like motionless fireflies. At the desk Roberts was seated, his flabby face worried, a stack of papers scattered around him.

'If you're the head of a deputation make an appointment,' he snapped. 'I'm about damned well sick of seeing cold light victims. You make the twentieth today. Come back tomorrow when my secretary can take the particulars. She isn't here now.'

'I know,' Sid replied quietly, and remained where he was.

Something in his voice made Roberts come to attention. He peered intently into the gloom beyond the desk light radiance.

'Come forward. Can't you? It annoys me talking to a face without a body.'

Sid obeyed, removing his hat as he did so. Roberts sat motionless in his chair, gazing at the merciless face in the midst of the cold light radiance.

'Sidney Cassell!'

'Right,' Sid agreed calmly. 'Next time you employ a strong-arm man to kill me make sure he does the job properly. As it is, the positions are reversed. I'm going to kill you now that I have completely wrecked your cold light industry.'

'Wrecked it? What the devil are you talking about? You haven't done anything of the sort! I'm still doing quite well and — '

'Don't try to tell me that, Roberts! People are after your blood, because they think your lamps are responsible for their being cold light victims. *I* am responsible for that, and I got the idea by accident. Come to think of it I could trace it back to being thrown in that copper mine. However, none of that signifies now. I'm here to kill you because you deserve it, as far as I'm concerned. Nobody will blame me because thousands are after your hide, and every one of them is luminous. So why should I be picked upon as the killer? See how nicely I have it worked out?'

Roberts got up and began to back round his desk. 'Now wait a minute, Cassell! You've got the facts all wrong. It was Grimsby Tate's idea to finish you off and — '

'Stop lying!' Sid cut in. 'It was you who gave the order to your strong-arm men. I was in the laboratory at the time. You called me the human glow-worm, remember?'

Roberts breathed hard. 'You can't do anything to me, Cassell. There's a night staff on the ground floor and you'll never get out without being seen.'

'I know all about the night staff. I got in without being seen and I'll go out the same way. Just the same, though,' Sid went on slowly, 'maybe I'll make a deal with you.'

'Anything!' Roberts exclaimed eagerly. 'Name it!'

'Cut me in for seventy-five per cent of the returns on this cold light game and I'll not kill you.'

'Seventy five per cent! That would make you the controlling factor!'

'I discovered cold light, didn't I? Stop fooling around, Roberts. Do you want to live, or don't you? Draw up a contract — I don't care how rough — and we'll sign it. In the morning it can be legalized properly.'

A swift thought appeared to pass through Roberts's mind. He gave a nod and relaxed somewhat.

'All right. You have me in a corner, but I'm the kind of man who's willing to buy himself out of a jam.'

'For this cold light you must have a formula,' Sid added. 'As controlling partner I want that, too. Get it.'

'But — '

'Get it!'

Scowling, Roberts went to his safe and opened it. He came back to the desk with a stiff sheet of parchment paper and its accompanying envelope. Sid took the formula and glanced over it.

'Where is Tate's?' he asked briefly. 'He must have had one to safeguard himself, surely? From what I've gathered of the facts you had him killed so he couldn't be your partner. So he must have had a formula.'

'He did. It was in the bank. Scotland Yard have it now.'

Sid narrowed his eyes. 'What the hell have Scotland Yard got to do with it?'

'Everything. Tate was murdered and I

had a fool of an inspector called Hodge badgering me for quite some time. He said the Yard had removed the formula from Tate's bank and it was already known that Tate was my partner. Fact remains the Yard could not pin anything on me, but if you want Tate's copy you'd better ask the Yard for it. Yet I don't think you will.'

'What I'll do is no business of yours, Roberts. At least I have this formula and that's my main concern. Cold light is my secret and nobody else's. As for the partnership contract between us you can forget it.'

'Forget it? But I thought — '

'You don't think I'd make a contract with a swine like you, do you? I'm perfectly aware you could find holes in a contract like that, and it would be more than my life is worth to wait for the morning to get the thing made legal. My only reason was to get you to hand over the formula. Now I have it I can settle my account.'

'But you said — '

'Never mind what I said. It's what I'm

going to do that counts.'

Roberts stood staring, expecting a gun to come into view. Instead Sid merely raised his hands. They were glowing weirdly, the fingers outspread — then with lightning speed he suddenly lashed them forward, seized Roberts by the throat, and bore him back against the desk.

Roberts had no idea what happened then. The terrific electrical shock he got paralyzed him, though he was strong enough a man not to lapse completely into unconsciousness — at least not to commence with. It was only when he realized the hands were crushing like steel bands that he made a desperate effort to save himself.

But he had not the strength. He lurched and struggled, but the hands never left him. Sid held on relentlessly until the gross body had tumbled sideways and collapsed on the carpet. Even then he kept his iron grip until he was satisfied the big fellow had stopped breathing. When this fact was at last established Sid slowly stood up, breathing hard.

To have disposed of Denham Roberts was one thing, but there was another matter also connected with Roberts to still be settled. The strong-arm man had to be found, the one who was always so apologetic. Sid's eyes slit at the thought of him and the memory of the push in the face he had received. The trouble was he did not know the man's name, but there might be a clue in the office here somewhere.

So Sid began to search, scattering papers far and wide. It was quite some time before it dawned on him there might be a possibility in the private line 'phone on the desk. It was obviously not directly connected to the exchange. If, at the other end of the line, there was the unmistakable voice of the strong-arm man, then —

Sid picked up the 'phone, and listened. A momentary pause and then, 'Yes, sir?'

'Come to my office at once,' Sid ordered, pitching his voice into the throaty guttural that Roberts had possessed. There came a muttered response from the other end as the strong-arm murmured something to a companion about settling some outstanding points with the 'old man.' Then Sid rang off.

He had no idea how far the henchman had to come, so he prepared himself to wait. He put his formula in his pocket, dragged the dead body of Roberts out of sight behind the desk then took up a position immediately behind the door, his fingers taut for action. He preferred his hands to weapons; they made no noise and they were immensely strong from his many years as a pylon engineer where sometimes his very life had depended on the strength of his fingers and wrists.

After perhaps ten minutes there came a knock on the door. Sid tensed himself.

'Come in,' he growled, and the door opened. He only needed a split second to satisfy himself that the man was the one he wanted — a fact he had already accepted from the voice — and then he sprang.

Not in the least expecting the onslaught, Drew was taken by surprise, but he rallied quickly to lash out with his powerful fists.

Sid dodged some of the blows, but not all of them. He took stinging punches to the head and face, but they were only transitory because the shock Drew had received at the outset had taken all the strength out of his muscles, and the more he touched Sid, or the more Sid touched him, the less power he had to act or think coherently. So at last Sid maneuvered the thug into the position he wanted, beside the great window. By this time Drew was too dazed to be conscious of what was actually happening, and Sid himself was too tired with the struggle to pursue his strangling tactics.

In consequence there thudded to the pavement one hundred and fifty feet below a man who was even then almost dead. The impact finished him and Sid leaned out, looking into the glare of cold light below and at the people who had swiftly gathered. He did not waste any more time.

Hurrying from the office he fled along the corridor and ran up the first emergency staircase he came to. As he had hoped it brought him out on the flat roof. The rest was not difficult. Accustomed to heights and toe-and-finger holds he was over the parapet and swinging onto the nearest power-line brackets within a matter of minutes. After that a swift descent to the rear of Roberts' edifice, where there was nobody about, and then onwards through the back alleys and unfrequented ways until he was well clear of danger.

He arrived back at his room in the East End with the feeling that he had accomplished much; but the moment he entered the room and switched on the light his expression changed. A stranger was seated in the shabby armchair, hat on his knees.

'Who the devil — ' Sid paused and closed the door slowly.

'You'll forgive the intrusion, I hope?' The man rose and held out his warrant-card. 'Your landlady had little choice. I wanted to make sure you wouldn't take fright before I had the chance to speak to you. You are Mr. Sidney Cassell, of course?'

Sid had nodded before he realized it. It

was just dawning on him that the name 'Hodge' on the warrant card was the same one that Roberts had used, Chief Inspector Hodge of Scotland Yard.

'Well, what do you want with me?' Sid asked brusquely.

'To clear up a few puzzling points, Mr. Cassell. I have had the devil of a job tracing you, particularly as you were, to all intents and purposes, dead. However, diligence on our part has at last been rewarded.'

'Oh, come to the point!' Sid snapped. 'And for your own sake keep your distance from me. I'm as electrical as a high voltage wire, like the rest of the cold light victims in this city.'

'Are you sure you are like the rest?' Hodge asked quietly.

'Eh? Course I'm sure.'

'I'm not — and that is why I am here. Scotland Yard has been ordered by the Government to look into this cold light affair which is spreading like a plague through the city — indeed through the country — and causing such trouble and panic everywhere. Many factors led me to seek you out because I knew long ago that you were the original cold light man, supposedly dead.'

'Well?'

'When other people began to have the same trouble, and I was told to investigate, I had scientists examine some of the cold light victims. One of the scientists thus employed was a Dr. Craymond and he — '

'Gave me away!'

'If you call it that.' Hodge sat down again. 'He told me you were alive; told me all about you, about a peculiar plan of vengeance you had worked out. Finally he told me that your being impregnated with copper had probably caused the cold light trouble to spread, notably to a doctor in the West Country. I had little difficulty in tracing that doctor since most of the folk in that village are outstanding by being luminous. At that time it was a phenomenon, but it wouldn't be now. So, then, it did not seem very difficult to assume that the trouble spreading like wildfire amongst the people of this city had been deliberately started by you.

Craymond said that was a scientific possibility because you had reached maximum emanation of cold light energy and therefore could transmit it to other living objects. Inorganic objects, like the lights themselves do not transmit their power to organic objects. So you see, it became quite obvious you were the culprit.'

'So now what?'

'I have to take you into custody, charged with being a menace to the security of the public.'

Sid laughed slightly. 'How do you propose doing it? Lay a hand on me and you'll get an electric shock sufficient to kill you.'

'I'm hoping you'll come quietly, Mr. Cassell. If you don't, there are other ways.'

'Name them!' Sid snapped.

Hodge did not respond, but he looked at a point just beyond Sid. Struck by the action, Sid twirled round, just in time to receive a noose that settled squarely over his shoulders. Before he could drag himself free the noose had tightened, pinning his arms to his sides. Without touching him, two P.C.s, who had evidently been hiding behind the bed, rapidly roped him up.

'All very unorthodox,' Hodge admitted, 'but then the situation itself is hardly normal. Right, boys — onto the stretcher with him.'

Completely helpless, Sid watched as a stretcher was brought from inside the wardrobe. Bound as he was, a pull on the ropes was sufficient to topple him helplessly onto the canvas. A sheet from the bed was thrown completely over him and that was that.

5

The formula destroyed

Sid was not released until he was in a prison cell, and then he had warders wearing specially insulated suits to deal with him. He fought and struggled savagely against them, but they were so well protected he was powerless to deliver any shocks. So finally they left him, sitting on his bunk and breathless with fury and exertion. It was bad enough to be imprisoned, but worse still that his precious cold light formula, along with other possessions he had had, had been taken from him into police custody.

Having nailed down the main cause of the cold light trouble, Hodge went further under Government instructions. The formula he had taken from Sid, together with the one which had belonged to Grimsby Tate, were both destroyed and a ban was placed on the sale of all further cold light lamps. Those in existence were to be removed and normal lighting restored.

'Not that I agree with any of it, sir,' Hodge protested to the Assistant Commissioner. 'The cold lamps themselves are quite harmless, and to have them removed robs humanity of one of the greatest boons it has ever known.'

The A.C. shrugged. 'No affair of mine, I'm afraid. I am merely acting under Government orders. The Government is quite convinced that the mounting number of cold light victims is caused by the lamps, even though we know that the original cause was Sidney Cassell. In other countries, where there are no cold light victims as yet — obviously because Sidney Cassell has not spread his malign influence that far — they are acting just as we are doing, not because they've had trouble but because they expect it.'

'Then something's got to be done about it.' Hodge decided. 'I'm not going to be a party to wiping out the greatest discovery of the age just because of a Government misconception of the facts.'

So Hodge took himself to Dr. Craymond and laid the facts before him. The physicist's alarm at the development of the situation was more than obvious.

'But does the Government realize what it is doing?' he demanded. 'Cold light has come to stay! It's got to stay because it is the most marvelous advance in lighting which ever happened. To destroy the formula for it is plain vandalism!'

'They've done it, and they're adamant,' Hodge answered. 'I myself saw the formula destroyed. I'm afraid I can't possibly convince the Government that cold lamps in themselves are quite harmless, so I've come to you. If things go on like this the Government is liable to destroy all cold lamps as well — make a clean sweep of everything. That'll mean the end of one of the finest discoveries of the age.'

Craymond gave the Yard man a vague look of surprise. 'Your dismay at the loss of a scientific discovery rather astonishes me, Inspector. I would have thought that a scientific invention would not have the slightest interest to you.'

'On the contrary. The Yard is always dealing with scientific equipment in these advanced days, and I hope I'm intelligent enough to appreciate the value of cold light. Anyway, it certainly ought not to be lost, and I don't want to continue being a party to its elimination.'

Craymond was silent for a while, then he gave a slow smile.

'Come to think of it,' he said finally, 'there's no need to worry. *Let* the Government drive cold light clean off the earth. Let them burn the formula! It doesn't matter.'

Hodge frowned. 'Doesn't matter?'

'Not with thousands of cold light victims walking the city at this moment. Any one of them can be analyzed here and the basic wavelength that causes their condition can be found. Simply repeat the experiment that was originally made on Sidney Cassell. Fortunately he is no longer unique; I can take my pick from anybody.'

'Yes, I suppose so,' Hodge agreed, surprised he had not thought of this answer before. 'But even supposing it is successful, the Government won't permit cold light to return to public life — so what good will it be?'

Craymond smiled. 'My dear man, all the Governments on Earth cannot prevent the development of a scientific discovery. For a year or two maybe cold light will be taboo, but at the right time it will come back. The Physical Research laboratory will go to work to prove that cold light itself is not a danger, and that Cassell was the predisposing cause of all the trouble. Once he is out of the way I'll wager cold light will resume, and *this* time the returns will come to me.'

'You? Not the Physical Laboratory as a body?'

'The Physical Laboratory is not primarily interested in commercial enterprise — but I am. If I am satisfied with the analysis I make, in the name of the Physical Laboratory, then I shall form a company to put cold light back again in such a way that no Government can interfere. You'll see. By that time Denham Roberts will be completely out of the picture.'

'Maybe, but the patent will still be his.'

'I shall use scientific variations in my system which will obviate any infringement of his rights. All I have to do now,' Craymond finished, his surprising revelation of business acumen evidently over, 'is find a volunteer.'

'Let me know how you get on,' Hodge said. 'I might even be interested in a partnership in this proposed company of yours.' Craymond only smiled, without further committing himself, and Hodge took his departure. When he arrived back at his dingy office in Whitehall it was to the information that Denham Roberts's body had been discovered — a victim of manual strangulation — and that there were also many puzzling features concerning the death of a man who had fallen from a window of Roberts's office. Thus, whilst higher authority's moves slowly extinguished cold lamps all over Britain, Scotland Yard investigated straightforward murder — and Dr. Craymond put out a request for a cold light volunteer.

To this there was no response, so — feeling much reassured of ultimate possibilities, thanks to the death of Denham Roberts — Craymond added a monetary bait out of his own pocket, and within an hour of the advertisement appearing in the press twenty men and women offered themselves.

Craymond selected the strongest looking man and promptly went into action, working now with the blessing of Sir Devenish Rondel; and, in his own sphere of activity, Chief Inspector Hodge was also busy, gathering together facts which inexorably pointed to Sidney Cassell as the murderer of Denham Roberts. Fingerprints, the testimony of witnesses who had seen him entering the Roberts building, his very clear thumb print on the telephone when he had called the strong-arm man: the case against him was quite complete. The facts in regard to Drew were not so clear — but in any event Sid was told by his 'insulated' defense lawyer that the charge against him was now murder as well as endangering public safety.

'Which doesn't worry me in the least,' Sid retorted.

The lawyer was silent, his face impassive behind the visor of his insulated suit. Speech was only possible by the audiophone on the front of his breastplate.

'All right,' Sid amended, sitting down again heavily on his bunk, 'so I'm talking like a fool . . . On the other hand I seem to get such a raw deal lately, that — Oh hell, what's the use!'

'Now perhaps you'll let *me* say something,' the lawyer intervened. 'Things are going to be tough for you; no doubt about that, and the only point I can work on is to show how you were victimized and nearly murdered through the orders of Denham Roberts. That may help matters. Give me the outline — every little detail, relevant or irrelevant.'

So, as calmly as he could, Sid gave all the facts. By the time he had finished he was morose again.

'Something damned ironic about all this,' he muttered. 'I brought about the death of Jim Prescott, my mate on the maintenance job, because he stood in my way where Mary Carter was concerned. I got away with that; everybody was satisfied it was an accident. Then when I got Mary she sold me out to Denham Roberts. Because of that I murdered him, and that brings me up to date. Funny how things catch up, isn't it?'

'One murder charge is sufficient to worry about at the moment,' the lawyer answered. 'I've got the details, and when your trial takes place I'll do all I can.'

Sid did not comment. Moodily he watched the lawyer depart. At about this time Dr. Craymond was at the close of his cold light experiment upon the volunteer. The man, a husky, thick-chested individual well over six feet tall, stood buttoning up his shirt over his glowing skin. At the deep preoccupation of Craymond he was obviously puzzled.

'What's the matter, doc?' he asked finally. 'Don't I qualify for that fee you offered?'

'Eh?' Craymond started. 'Yes, of course you do. You shall have it before you leave. I'm just a little perplexed, that's all. Tell me, where did you first develop this cold light phenomenon?'

'No idea. It just sort of happened. One day I found I was red, like the wife had been for some time, then it just went on developing until it finished up white, like it is now. I was scared at first, but not any more. Doesn't seem to do me any harm. I feel a hundred per cent as far as health is concerned.'

Craymond was silent. The man's expression slowly changed.

'Look here, what sort of an end do you get with this ailment — if you can call it that? Is it painful?'

'No. Once it has reached maximum it stays there and does no more harm than the natural reflection of light from the skin. Even the genuine case of cold light 'disease' is not dangerous when at maximum, as has been proved by the case of Sidney Cassell, the original cold light man. In the spurious form the cold light will probably die out gradually as the balance is adjusted.'

'Die out!' The man looked astonished. 'You mean I'll get better? Go normal with no more glowing?'

'It's possible,' Craymond replied absently; then he brisked up again. 'Here is your check, my friend, and thank you for offering yourself. You have proved invaluable to scientific research.'

Craymond wasted no further time getting rid of his volunteer, then he made his way quickly to the office of Sir Devenish Rondel to report on his activities.

'The most extraordinary thing, Sir Devenish!' Craymond exclaimed, the moment he was in the office. 'The cold light effect on normal people appears to be spurious.'

'Spurious?' the physicist repeated, astonished. 'Cold light is cold light, Dr. Craymond. There cannot be two versions of the same thing.'

'So I would say — as a scientist. But the fact remains that my tests of our volunteer show that his molecular set-up is entirely normal. The glow he is radiating, though it goes through all the stages common to cold light — as evidenced by Sidney Cassell — is nothing more than a discharge of energy which, having reached the maximum emanation, will now start to diminish.'

'You mean that all the hundreds of people who have apparently cold light phenomena have really not got it at all?'

'Not the real thing. Apparently only Sidney Cassell has that.' Craymond sat down and continued urgently. 'The position as I see it is this: Cassell, by contact, gave that doctor in the West country some kind of an electrical shock due to his — Cassell's — own extraordinary condition. The effect did not change the doctor's molecular set-up but it did charge him with a form of energy similar to that imparted, which is of course a natural law of physics. Like produces like. The energy, in dissipating, produced all the known characteristics of cold light, but it is not the actual thing. It was handed on to others. Thousands of people in the city here contracted it due to Cassell's machinations, but it still is not genuine.'

Rondel mused through an interval and then sighed. 'Yet how very natural,' he said at length. 'In the field of radiation we get all manner of counterfeits of the original radiation, even to the 'echo' of radio waves, so that cold light should produce a useless ghost of itself is not perhaps so fantastic. A great pity, Dr. Craymond, a great pity.'

'It's more than a pity, Sir Devenish, it's a tragedy!' Craymond exclaimed. 'Don't you realize what it means? The only source of cold light we have left is Sidney Cassell himself, and he is to stand trial for murder! And he'll certainly be sentenced. The most valuable man to science who ever lived, and the law is out to put him away for life.'

'Yes, I appreciate the position,' Sir Devenish responded after a moment. 'All formulae destroyed, all lamps themselves removed — '

'The lamps themselves can never tell us anything,' Craymond interrupted. 'They are merely adjusted molecularly to a particular set-up which produces cold light: It is the exciting cause we have to get. And Cassell has it.'

'I'll see if there is anything I can do,' Rondel said. 'We can't have so valuable a secret eluding us.'

But as far as the law was concerned Sir Devenish Rondel was less than the dust and no pleadings on his part from the scientific angle could persuade the authorities to release Sidney Cassell from imprisonment, not even for the purposes of a test. Having thus failed, Sir Devenish gave up the battle — but not Dr. Craymond. He had a commercial stake in the whole idea if he could only get Sid in his laboratory for about five minutes: so he enlisted the aid of all the most famous scientists in the world, getting their signature to a petition asking for the release of Sidney Cassell, under police supervision throughout, in the name of science. This had an effect. Since science was going to be bereft of a highly important secret, and since police supervision could be maintained throughout, something could perhaps be done. Then, at the last moment, the highest authorities in criminal law turned down the application.

Had his stake in the proceedings not been such a high one Craymond would probably have then retired from the fight — but he still had not finished. He petitioned the Government itself and at first met with polite interest and nothing more.

Then, gradually, Craymond drove home his point to those officials who had been responsible for the ruthless destruction of all things concerned with cold light. It was shown to them as a scientific fact that cold light itself was not a danger, that those people who had the 'disease' would very soon become normal again. In a word, the blame for destroying the most valuable discovery of the decade was placed firmly on the Government. It could only save its face by permitting Sidney Cassell's release for experiment.

Big-wig conferred with big-wig; there were conferences behind closed doors, at some of which the Assistant Commissioner of Scotland Yard's criminal department was present — and at last it was agreed that Sidney Cassell should have three hours' absence from jail, provided always he was accompanied by armed warders, armed in this case because of the extraordinary nature of their prisoner.

The man given the task of explaining the situation to Sid Cassell was the man who had run him in — Chief Inspector Hodge. When he arrived, protected, as were all visitors and warders, by an insulated suit, Hodge found Sid sprawled on his bunk, the radiance from him visible even in the dim daylight through the cell window.

'Oh — you!' Sid said, recognizing the face through the visor, and he deliberately turned over so that he showed his back.

'Special news for you, Cassell,' Hodge said. 'You are to be given a chance to redeem yourself.'

'From what?'

'From the charges against you. You'll improve your chances a lot if you hand to science the very thing you have been using as a weapon of vengeance.'

Sid turned over and sat up. 'What the hell are you talking about?' he demanded bluntly.

'Cold light. Dr. Craymond wishes to analyze you, and the authorities have granted permission.'

'And what does that make me?'

'A benefactor instead of an enemy of society.'

Sid grinned cynically. 'What kind of a fool do you take me for? No matter what I give to science I'll still be convicted at the trial.'

'There's a chance you may not be if you do this — and there is a monetary consideration in it too, according to Dr. Craymond.'

'Craymond, eh? I thought you mentioned him. You can tell him from me he can go straight to the Milky Way and stop there. If he offered me fifty millions and my freedom this minute I'd still say the same.'

'But you can't! Dammit, man, can't you see I'm trying to help you — '

'You're not trying to help *me*,' Sid interrupted. 'You are trying to help yourself and Dr. Craymond. And for that there has to be a reason. Obviously it's my cold light affliction. Why bother me when thousands of people have got the same thing? Why try and turn me from a common criminal into a national hero?'

'Thousands of other people *haven't* got the same thing: that's just the point! Their ailment is spurious whereas yours is genuine. You are the only man who possesses real cold light.'

Sid frowned. 'Spurious? How does that come about?'

'I don't know. Craymond did explain it to me but I'm not scientist enough to grasp it. The fact remains all formulae concerning cold light have been destroyed and most of the lamps jettisoned. Even the patent office has had to destroy their copy formula by Government order. What few lamps are left cannot tell anything and — '

Sid burst out into such hysterical laughter that Hodge came to a stop. He waited grimly whilst Sid recovered.

'If that doesn't beat everything!' Sid exclaimed. 'The masterminds grab the secret from me in the early stages, try to kill me, and then destroy everything concerning it. Now they think I'm mug enough to hand it back again. Not on your life! Think of the revenge I can get by withholding my secret, and once I am dead it won't be the least use to anybody. I learned that long ago. Molecular activity stops with death, and cold light will stop with it. I wouldn't help Dr. Craymond if he were the last man on Earth, not after the way he betrayed me to you.'

'Look, Cassell, you — '

'Leave me alone, can't you? You can't force this experiment upon me. I have rights even if I am in a prison cell.'

Behind the visor Hodge compressed his lips and then took his leave. He reported the interview to the Government and then to Dr. Craymond himself.

'This is monstrous,' Craymond muttered, clenching his fists. 'We just *can't* afford to lose this secret, Hodge. Something's got to be done.'

Hodge sighed. 'What, for instance? Nothing more I can do and you certainly can't spirit Cassell out of prison.'

Craymond paced around slowly for a while and then came to a stop. 'You know something of the facts ranged for and against Cassell. What do you think the verdict of the trial will be?'

'I'd say guilty — without hesitation.'

Craymond came forward. 'How far are you prepared to go, Hodge, to take up that partnership in cold light with me? I'm prepared to work fifty-fifty with you if you are prepared to sink everything, principles and career included, in order to get hold of Cassell.'

'I'd have to have a mighty strong guarantee of success before I'd sacrifice that much,' Hodge said, but there was a human waver in his voice just the same.

'Between us, my friend, we might legally obtain his release altogether — and notice I say *legally*. The charges against him are murder, and jeopardizing the safety of the public. I now have evidence, and so has the Government, that the malady afflicting the public is only a temporary and harmless one. If that fact is driven home by the defense — and I can give the lawyer all the facts — there is every chance that the charge may have to be dropped. When nobody is hurt the charge can't stand up. Right?'

'Possibly, but that's a trifle compared to the charge of murder. That's where he'll be nailed.'

'Not if you find fresh evidence, my friend.'

Hodge laughed shortly. 'Fresh evidence? There isn't any! I've been over the business with a toothcomb.'

'The best of us, police officers included, make mistakes. Now you know what I meant by your sacrificing your career, your principles, and everything else.' Craymond tapped the bench beside him. 'If you prove beyond a shadow of doubt that it was that strong-arm Drew who did the killing, and *not* Cassell, the possibility is that he will be released, or else serve a negligible sentence for the upset he created. Once we get that he's ours. We'll *make* him do as we want if we have to abduct him.'

Hodge bit his lip. He was in about the most difficult quandary of his life. From his own investigations he knew already the fabulous fortune which Denham Roberts had made in his brief career of cold light glory; therefore, even split in half by sharing with Craymond, there was no reason why such a fortune could not be made again, many times over with no opposition. On the other hand he would jettison all his honesty as a police officer and be a willing party, as far as he himself was concerned, to perjury.

'I can't do it,' he said abruptly.

Craymond grinned. 'That's your first reaction, of course. Consider the facts. Who would get the blame? The dead strong-arm man whom nobody cares about. Do you want your career and pension so much that you're willing to throw away millions? If you do the job properly nobody can ever know.'

'I've heard that said before, too,' Hodge muttered.

'If we don't do it Cassell will certainly be put away for life — and that will be the end of our El Dorado.'

'You forget that I didn't investigate the Roberts business on my own,' Hodge protested, moving around restlessly. 'I had Detective-Sergeant Bannerman with me, checking up on everything I found. He'll know I'm lying if I rake up fresh evidence.'

'You're trying to convince yourself, Hodge,' Craymond said. 'You've been in the business long enough to devise some false evidence if you wish — something that could easily have escaped Bannerman. I do not suggest you try to prove Cassell was never there; it is quite plain that he was, from fingerprints and witnesses. But he *could* have been forestalled by Drew, the strong-arm man. Work it out for yourself and let me know your decision.'

'All right,' Hodge replied moodily. 'I'll do my best.'

Craymond only smiled, knowing only too well the frailty of human nature. From the very first Hodge had revealed himself as more than interested in cold light than he was in the law: there seemed to be little doubt to Craymond what the result would be.

And he was right. That same evening Hodge called upon the physicist at his Surbiton home, and even before he spoke it was plain he had made up his mind.

'I'm going to take the risk,' he said bluntly. 'I also have a plan worked out. I've been checking back on Drew as a starter, and there's a piece of good luck in the evidence, which *could* be legitimate. Therefore I don't feel quite so badly about it. In plain language, Drew was not alone when he was told to come to Roberts's office. He had one of the other men with him and, re-reading his evidence, it seems that Drew told him Roberts wanted him.'

'Well?'

'The first point is that Roberts telephoned at a time when our pathological evidence shows that he should have been dead; and the other point is Drew said to his companion it would be a good chance to settle a lot of outstanding points with the old man. What he meant by that I don't know, nor does Drew's henchman, but the defense could probably twist it to show that Drew meant to have a showdown with his boss.'

'Very probably,' Craymond agreed. 'Anything else?'

'The marks on Roberts's neck were plainly from manual strangulation, but no pathologist would be able to swear to the fingerprints. They might have been marks made by either Drew or Cassell. I intend to play up the Drew angle, or rather the lawyer will. Lastly, witnesses saw Cassell enter the building, yes — but others also saw Drew enter it as well. On the other hand, Cassell was never seen to leave, so there might have been a mistake as to his entering. As for Drew we know what happened to him. His body was found on the pavement. I think the defense could make enough of the facts to shake the testimony against Cassell very considerably.'

6

Retribution

So Sid Cassell's case came to court, and he was perfectly aware through his defense lawyer of the fight that was going to be put up on his behalf. He had made no comment, and in court he certainly did not since it was not his place to do so. Standing between two insulated warders he listened to the back and forth arguments and occasionally looked at the judge.

For three days the wrangling of the law continued, and it became increasingly obvious that the defense was proving its point — so much so that, towards the end of the defense counsel's speech to the jury, Sid suddenly interrupted the proceedings with an unexpected outburst.

'M'lord, all this is a direct reversal of the facts! I did murder Denham Roberts, and in the same circumstances I would do it again — '

Uproar. Harsh words from the judge. His gavel thumped fiercely, but Sid refused to be silenced.

'All the defense is trying to do is release me, so that I can become a scientific tool with which to experiment!' Sid shouted. 'No matter what the defense proves, I am still a murderer. I didn't only kill Denham Roberts and Drew; I killed Jim Prescott as well a long time ago at the top of a pylon — '

'Will you be silent!' the judge thundered. 'Apart from everything else this court is only concerned with your responsibility in respect of the deaths of Denham Roberts and Amos Drew. Anything else you may say, or confess to, will be disregarded.'

'But, m'lud, I — '

Sid could get no further. The uproar was complete. Even the judge could not proceed and, with a vinegary look on his face, he cleared the court, suspending proceedings until the following day. On the resumption of the hearing the result was inevitable. After only a ten-minute retirement by the jury, Sid was found not guilty and promptly acquitted.

'Having regard to your extraordinary condition, Mr. Cassell,' the judge said, automatically restoring to Sid his name and prefix, 'you will not leave this court in the ordinary way for fear of contact with other people. I have made arrangements for the Electro-Physical Laboratory to be responsible for you which, in your condition, is the only logical move.'

'I will not go to the Electro-Physical Laboratory now, or ever,' Sid retorted, 'I'm a free man, and you cannot make me.'

'On the contrary. Mr. Cassell, kindly remember that you have only been acquitted of the charges brought against you. That in no wise renders you safe to mingle with society. Until you are fit to do so the Electro-Physical Laboratory will be in charge.'

Sid gave a grim took about him, but there was nothing he could do to evade the grip his insulated warders had upon him.

He was taken from the crowded courtroom down the empty, gloomy corridors and finally to the yard at the rear. Here he was placed in a plain van and had the door locked upon him. He was alone, but he could hear the murmur of voices. The glow from his face and hands illumined the darkness brightly.

Then with a jerk the van suddenly started on its way. Sid moved to the dense wooden partition between him and the driver, but there was no possible way of seeing who was in control. Sid had no need to be a genius to realize that the whole matter of 'responsibility for him' had been engineered by Dr. Craymond — and once in his grip at the Electro-Physical Laboratory there would be no way out.

As near as Sid could remember the Electro-Physical Laboratory was about two miles from the law courts, and through the thick of the city traffic, so he had a little while in which to decide his course of action and, slowly, an idea began to develop. Up to now he had never tried his electrical powers upon metals, though he knew he could generate a considerable voltage through them. Here was a case where it might be the means of his escape.

The notion had no sooner taken shape than he tugged off his trousers' belt and looked at the buckle, brightly lighted by the glow of his hands. Quickly he moved to the rear door and inserted the buckle down the thin partition where the doors did not quite meet. Gripping one end of the buckle he put the other end on the hasp of the padlock outside. Instantly the reaction against the metal made him jolt and gasp with pain. It felt as though a thin, pliant cane had been lashed across his fingers. But the hasp had parted, incinerated by the brief current he had driven through it. Automatically the glow of his body had correspondingly decreased, like a battery drained of its power. In time he would rebuild it, but this was not his immediate concern.

He worked upon the doors steadily and at length the padlock dropped away and he had the view of the road outside as the doors swung open. Just at the moment the van was not being followed by traffic, though there was plenty moving in the opposite direction.

Without hesitation he levered himself over the edge of the van and then let himself drop. The road surface whipped his feet from under him and he rolled over and over into the gutter. Immediately he was on his feet again and started running for the nearest side turning he could find. In five minutes he had stopped running, reasonably satisfied that he could not be pursued.

And now what? It dawned upon him at this moment — more clearly indeed than it had ever done before — that he was completely without a friend. Nor had he any money. All his personal belongings had been in the hands of the police and, presumably, would have been returned to him at the Electro-Physical Laboratory. As things were now he had only his own resources to rely on — to the tune of several hundred volts of electricity and an utterly reckless mood.

Acquitted, and yet a fugitive. The thing was fantastic. A fugitive from science. He preferred to die rather than give up his cold light secret to the very ones who had betrayed him to the law. Such was his personal way of looking at it, rooted as it was in complete self-centeredness and ignoring entirely that he was a killer three times over.

Perhaps there might yet be a fourth time! His mind switched abruptly to one whom he had not yet had the chance to deal with. Mary Carter! But for her none of this ghastly mess would ever have come about.

In the end he decided to use his deadly powers to full effect and throw everything he had got into a final effort to find Mary Carter and get his revenge. Thus it was that towards noon an unsuspecting businessman took a deserted side street for a short cut and abruptly found himself confronted by a haggard, dusty-looking man who emerged from the shadows of a disused garage. Since it was full daylight there was nothing to betray Sid's luminosity. The businessman gave him a glance, and then prepared to continue on his way.

'Just a moment!' Sid ordered, as the man came level.

'Well? I'm in a hurry.'

'So am I. You don't know me and I don't know you — '

'On the contrary. You're Sidney Cassell. I've seen your photograph in the papers a good deal recently. What you're doing here is no affair of mine so, if you'll allow me to pass — '

'I think not.' Sid shook his head, his face grim. 'I need money and decent clothes. I'm hoping you can give me the first and it's obvious you can give me the latter.'

Wasting no further time he grabbed the businessman by the throat as he made a sudden desperate effort to hurry on his way. The effect was immediate. Without a sound the man collapsed, his limbs twitching from the force of the electric shock he had received. Sid kept his hands about the man's throat until he was satisfied that life had ceased — then he dragged the body into the dim chaos of the ancient garage and quickly changed his clothes. In the businessman's pockets he found a fair quantity of money, in various denominations. So at length Sid emerged, looking remarkably respectable and relentlessly determined. Somewhere amidst the debris in the old garage was the body he had dispossessed.

He did not dare to lunch in a café in case it gave anybody the chance to study him at leisure and so determine who he was; so instead he bought a loaf and some fruit and made these suffice for the time being.

Meantime, at the Physical Laboratory, the escape of the 'prisoner' had been discovered. Dr. Craymond, usually so deadly calm, flew into a rage and stormed at the two men to whom he had entrusted the task.

'Idiots! Fools!' he shouted, pacing up and down the laboratory. 'Do you realize what you have done? There's no possible way of finding him because thousands of people in the city have all got glowing bodies just as he has. He might be anywhere — just anywhere! How the devil did it happen, anyway?'

'No idea,' growled the man who had

been the driver. 'When we arrived we found the doors of the van open and no sign of Cassell.'

Craymond tightened his lips then jerked his head. 'All right, get out. Evidently Cassell was too smart for you.'

The men left. Craymond meditated for a moment and then crossed to the 'phone. In a moment or two he was speaking to Hodge at Scotland Yard.

'Better come over as quick as you can, Hodge. We're in something of a mess. I can't explain over the 'phone.'

'Be there right away,' Hodge replied quickly, his voice startled — and in fifteen minutes he had arrived, to be quickly acquainted with the facts.

'So there it is,' Craymond finished bitterly. 'After all our plotting and planning we've lost him!'

'But he hasn't got to stay lost!' Hodge protested. 'Look at the way I sold myself out in court. Threw away my reputation because I relied implicitly on what you were going to do and — '

'Oh, shut up!' Craymond snapped. 'You can't blame me for this: it was those bungling fools driving the van who ought to be shot! Every damned thing fixed, even to the authorities agreeing to the Physical Laboratory acting as Cassell's 'guardian,' and this is what we get! I've told Sir Devenish because I had to.'

'And what did be say?'

'Nothing he *could* say. He simply accepts Cassell as lost and the organization thereby relieved of a heavy responsibility. I don't think even now that Rondel credits Cassell with being the sole possessor of cold light on this planet.'

For a moment or two there was silence; then Craymond said:

'The job's up to you from now on, Hodge. In your capacity you can put men on the job to trace Cassell. You have every reason for doing so because he's a public danger. Even a criminal lunatic would be innocuous compared to what Cassell can do in his present electrical state. Better get your authority from the Assistant Commissioner and then shift heaven and Earth. Cassell must be *found*!'

'I can try,' Hodge admitted dubiously. 'If only he alone were glowing it would be simple — but with hundreds of folk in a similar state I can't see my men getting far.'

'Your men have tracked criminals down before today: they can surely track Cassell. They'd better if either of us are ever going to cash in.'

Hodge gave a gloomy nod and took his departure, leaving Craymond fuming silently to himself. At this time also Sid Cassell, wearing dark glasses, and looking remarkably like a well-tailored solicitor suffering from eye trouble, had arrived at the rooming house where Mary Carter had at one time lived. The bosomy proprietress opened the front door to him.

'Good afternoon, madam.' Sid raised his stolen homburg briefly. 'I am — '

'We don't want any, thank you. Good day!'

'I am a solicitor, madam, seeking a young woman by the name of Mary Carter. I understand she lives here?'

'She did. She quit — owing me two weeks' rent, too. That was a long time ago.'

'And left no indication of where she was going?'

'Not she! I'd have been after 'er otherwise. Sorry, mister, I can't help you.'

'This is most unfortunate,' Sid sighed. 'She has come into quite a sizeable legacy and I must locate her. However — '

'Legacy?' The woman pricked up her ears, as Sid had hoped she would. 'That's interestin'. Maybe I could get my back rent if she could be located?'

'I would consider it very possible. The legacy is large enough to make Miss Carter independent for life. Why, do you think you might have some clue to her whereabouts?'

'*I* haven't, but she has a young man friend called Kenneth Lipscomb. He came here once lookin' for 'er, and he left his address. Maybe he can tell you something. Just a minute.'

Sid waited. Presently the woman returned and handed him a slip of paper on which an address was scrawled. 'There y'are, mister. Maybe that'll help. If you find 'er tell 'er I want my back rent, and quick.'

'Definitely I will,' Sid promised, and took his departure.

The address was in a somewhat dubious section of the East End. Sid wasted no time in going to it, no longer having any uneasiness in regard to his disguise. He was satisfied that he looked a legal man, and that if the authorities were on the watch for him they'd never spot him.

The East End address proved to be another cheap tenement house, little different from the one he had just left. He looked down the list of names at the front door and finally discovered 'Mr. and Mrs. Lipscomb — 5th Floor.'

Sid frowned to himself. The 'Mrs.' puzzled him, though of course it could well be that Kenneth Lipscomb was a 'double lifer' with Mary Carter on the side. Perhaps an enquiry or two first?

But there did not appear to be anybody present whom he could question. Certainly there was nobody in the narrow hall, and the various doors he tried on the lower floor brought forth no response. So at length he made up his mind and went up to the fifth floor. Here there was only one door, on a top landing, and a more dismal set-up it would be hard to find.

He knocked sharply on the solitary door, and waited.

After a moment or two it opened and to his amazement there was Mary Carter, a slut with a smudged face and lank hair tumbling over her forehead, looking out at him.

'What is it?' she demanded irritably. 'I'm busy cooking.'

'Your husband in?' Sid asked briefly, and at the sound of his voice, which he did not try to alter, he saw her expression change.

'He's — he's in, yes — '

Sid jammed his foot in the doorway. 'Don't try and fool me, Mary. If he is in I'll deal with him.'

His shoulder pushed the door wide against her resistance and in another moment he was inside the drab room. It was poorly furnished, faded washing hung on lines. The walls were defiled with damp marks.

'It's you, Sid, it's you!' Mary backed

away towards the window, then came up hard against it.

'Right!' Sid took off his dark glasses and put them in his breast pocket. Then he looked about him. 'Where's your husband?'

'He's not here. He's out at work. I — Sid, I know what you are thinking.'

'No you don't, else you'd jump through that window. I'm giving you warning. Mary. Don't touch me or you'll drop dead. That's what cold light's done for me.'

'I know. I read all about you in the papers.' Mary was breathing hard now and it made Sid smile tautly as he saw the fear in her eyes.

'Did you also read that I escaped my 'guardians' — the magnanimous Electro-Physical Laboratory — especially to find you?'

'No. No, I didn't.'

Silence. Sid measuring her with relentless eyes.

'Doesn't seem to have done you much good, the money you got for betraying me into Denham Roberts's hands, does it?'

‘It wasn’t much. I got through it in double quick time and then came back to London. I — I finally married Ken Lipscomb. He’d always been pestering me. Then he got out of work and we came down to this. He’s only just found a job again.’

‘Uh-huh. Y’know, Mary, this is mighty lucky, my finding you like this. I’d expected I’d have to tramp half over Britain, or even go to the Continent, to locate you. Instead you’re right here — and you can’t get away, either. No more than I could when Roberts’s boys were around me. Remember?’

Mary made an uncertain movement and then settled back again beside the window. Her back was to the light, which made Sid’s merciless face all the clearer.

‘You’re the last one, Mary,’ he said.

‘Last one?’

‘Uh-huh. I dealt with Roberts and the man who pushed me into the copper mine. That left only you. I was delayed in getting to you, but I’m here now. You sold me out. Mary, and I’ve never forgotten it.’

‘But I — ’

'Shut up while I'm talking! I murdered Jim Prescott — because of you. I lost the chance of ten million pounds — because of you. I nearly lost my life — because of you. Now I'm pursued, not by the law so much as by scientists who want my secret for nothing! Why? Once again, because of you. But this time it's going to be different. In this city there are something like four or five thousand people all glowing like fireflies in the night, and I'm only one of them. I can never be exactly identified. I'm going to kill you, Mary, and leave you so it looks like a straightforward electric shock. Later I'm going to build up the mightiest business in cold light the world has ever seen. Science isn't getting my secret! Nobody's getting it except me! If you hadn't been such a fool it could have you as well. But not now, Mary.'

'I know I did wrong,' Mary said, coming forward urgently. 'I just couldn't help it when Roberts dangled all that money before me. I couldn't think straight and — '

'You thought straight enough to ditch

me and let me think you loved me. That's one thing no real man can stand: being had for a mug. Come here!'

Mary made to draw back but in that instant Sid had grasped her tightly by her shoulders. She quivered a little, but nothing more. Wide-eyed, she stood looking at him.

'Why the devil are you standing like that?' Sid yelled at her.

'Why shouldn't I?' she asked. 'You're holding me.'

'Yes, but — ' A look of blank consternation crossed Sid's face. He removed his hands from her shoulders and instead put them about her neck. She remained looking at him fixedly and, somehow, she did not look afraid any more.

'This is incredible,' he whispered, lowering his hands and staring at her. 'You, the one I have most reason to hate, and you don't drop dead before the electrical force I'm radiating. I've killed strong men by merely touching them, yet you — ' Sid rubbed his face slowly. 'It's beyond reason.'

'You were once an electrical maintenance engineer, Sid,' Mary told him. 'Have you forgotten all you ever learned at that job? Remember how you and Jim Prescott used to talk about the different resistances of people? How one man — Big Mike, you called him — used to be able to grab a five-hundred-volt feeder line and join it up without batting an eyelash?'

'Yes, but — ' Sid jolted suddenly. 'Good God, you don't mean you have an extra strong resistance to electricity?'

'Looks like it, doesn't it? I'm no electrician, but from what you've told me I know some people can absorb a terrific current without trouble, whereas others go out instantly at a mere low voltage shock.' Mary moved away to the dismal window. 'Ever since I was a kid I can remember electricity never frightened me. I've poked my fingers in a live lamp socket and only had a tingle.'

Sid stood staring at her, unbelieving. To make sure he strode across and grabbed her again, but nothing happened.

'That's it, resistance,' he whispered.

'The very thing I never thought of. So far I've never found anybody who could stand up to my voltage. Why the hell does it have to be you?'

'I don't know. I can't help the way I'm made.'

Sid swung away, driving his fist into his palm in vexation.

'Spoils your plan, doesn't it?' Mary asked dryly. 'You can't fix me with an electrical shock because I don't 'take' to it properly.'

'There are other ways. I could choke the life out of you. I could — ' Sid stopped and said surprisingly, 'Maybe it's a sign, Mary.'

'Of what?'

'That I'm not meant to destroy you. Yes, I know the sort of hatred I've built up against you since you sold me out, but deep down I've sort of loved you as well. I wouldn't have got Jim Prescott out of the way if I didn't really love you, would I?'

Mary did not say anything. She continued looking out if the window on the dismal scene. Then Sid wandered back to her side. 'The longing for revenge is a hellish thing,' he whispered. 'Even worse when it doesn't materialize in the finish. In this case I'm glad it hasn't. I'd have been pretty lonely with those millions all by myself. It isn't going to be just mere millions in the future, though. It'll be a vaster fortune, piled sky-high. What do you say we forget all the mistakes and start again?'

Mary stirred and gazed at him. 'I've married in the interval, Sid. You're forgetting that.'

'Before morning's here you'll be a widow. I'll see to that. Unless you married a man as resistant to electricity as yourself. Do you love this mug Lipscomb?'

'No. He was doing all right when I took him on; now we're down to this.' Mary sighed. 'A fortune, just to forget all that has happened. I'd love it, Sid, because comfort is all I'm looking for. It's all I've ever looked for!'

'Then why the hell did you sell me out to Roberts when I was about set to clean up a pile?'

'Because that pile was not sure and

Roberts's thousands were. Bird in the hand. You know how it is.' Mary's eyes hardened a little. 'Listen, Sid, I may be unreliable: I may play one man against another and take money where I can see it waiting to be picked up — but I'll not be a party to murder. You talk of wiping out Ken. I won't stand for that. If you think we can sort ourselves out by starting again then let's go and leave Ken to work it out for himself.'

'Why this sudden highly-developed attack of scruples?' Sid demanded sourly. 'What's one man more — or woman — as far as I'm concerned? I've wiped out six or seven as it is.'

'That's on your conscience, not mine. I will not be a party to Ken's destruction. Not because I love him but because I have that spark of humanity left in me.'

Sid reflected and sat down slowly on one of the rickety chairs. 'Okay, we'll have it your way. We'll leave now.'

'No — not right away, Sid. We need something to eat first. You look pretty tired.'

'I am.' Sid looked at her listlessly. 'All

right — soon as we've had something.'

At that she turned away and busied herself laying a meal. Sid watched the proceedings, not speaking, his mind dwelling upon the queer turn things had taken. He had a curious let-down feeling. He had built up everything to the point of killing Mary, only to find she was still here and, for some reason which he could only assume was fundamentally biological, as attractive as she had always been. He did not see the slovenly appearance, the untidy clothes. He saw only Mary and realized that he still wanted her.

'Drink this,' she said at last, and handed him a cup of tea.

He took it, drank it slowly, and then turned to the sandwiches of meat paste that she had prepared. He did not remember finishing them, but he did remember finding himself on his back on a roughly-made bed, his eyes staring at a faded ceiling.

'What the devil — ?' he muttered to himself, and struggled into a sitting position. He was in a bedroom of sorts, its furniture extremely ordinary, the view through the smudged window revealing slate roofs cut up into bleak segments.

How had this happened? From the feeling of his aching head he had been drugged or something. He was just about to call to Mary when a voice stopped him. It was a man's, and for the moment he thought it was somebody in the next room, then from its mechanical intonation he realized it was coming from a radio. In a confused, head-heavy way he sat on the edge of the bed, listening.

'Repeat warning! Attention all listeners! Sidney Cassell the cold light man, is still at large. It is possible, from the latest information to hand, that he will be dressed like a city businessman. Be on your guard; this man is dangerous Notification of his whereabouts should be given to the nearest police station or to Dr. Craymond of the Electro-Physical Laboratory. Repeat: this man is dangerous. A reward of twenty thousand pounds for information concerning him will — '

Suddenly the voice stopped and the radio snapped off. Sid looked up slowly, his eyes narrowing. He shook his head to clear it of the fog and then lurched over to the window. He noticed immediately that the day was much further advanced than it had been when he had started on the sandwiches. He noticed something else, too: a police patrol car drawing up on the other side of the street, from which two men alighted.

Immediately the whole set-up dawned upon him. He swung, the fogs of drug clearing out of his head, and yanked open the door. Mary was in the room beyond, looking very much as before, except that her slow, nervous pacing revealed how much she was consumed by anxiety.

At Sid's abrupt appearance, and the expression on his face her hand flew momentarily to her mouth in alarm.

'Clever, aren't you?' Sid spat at her. 'I heard that warning on the radio, and it isn't very difficult to guess the rest. That warning was a repeat, implying it's been given before — no doubt while I was wandering through the city. That reward had been offered before I arrived here, hadn't it?

Mary was silent, gripping the edge of

the table, her eyes wide.

'Hadn't it?' Sid demanded, striding across to her. 'Thought you'd get smart, didn't you? Drugged me, and then told the police. They're just arriving across the road. Can't ever play the game straight, can you?'

'Look, Sid, you've got it all wrong — '

'Sounds like it, doesn't it?' he demanded, as there came the noise of heavy feet in the corridor outside. 'I'm satisfied now, Mary. You're clean rotten right through. Not content with selling me out once you've tried to do it again. Pity for you my constitutional change evidently made me recover earlier than normal from whatever you gave me in that tea.'

Sid did not give her the chance to answer. At a pounding on the door he gave a desperate glance about him — and saw the heavy old poker lying in the dirty grate. He whipped it up, then slammed it down, three times. At the sound of the door being gradually smashed inwards from the impact of heavy shoulders he dived for the window, whipped it open, and took a flying leap to the nearest roof. Then he was on his way, leaping from parapet to parapet, until at last he saw an empty wagon yard below him. To scramble to it by way of a drainpipe was simple. Then he continued on his way.

There were no sounds of pursuit, though here and there in this quiet side street men and women passed singly and gave him a curious glance. He straightened his hair, smoothed out his dusty suit, and continued at a more leisurely pace. For the moment he had forgotten that he had money. Then when it finally dawned on him he called a passing taxi and dived into it.

The thing to do now was to get somewhere quiet. Somewhere perhaps where there was not radio or television. Then, when the hue and cry had subsided, he could emerge again, untraceable because he glowed as much as any of the thousands of the victims in the city. He must change his clothes, his appearance . . .

* * *

But, even whilst Sid was laying his plans to drop out of sight, there was a scientific change taking place amongst the thousands who had been afflicted with spurious cold light. Stated simply, the effect was dying out. Having reached a maximum output the queer, counterfeit cold light reaction was waning, even as a star sometimes wanes after an outburst of furious energy.

The news was transmitted to all scientific quarters the moment it became apparent, and of course to Dr. Craymond. The first thing he did was to send for Chief Inspector Hodge, and though it was close on ten o'clock and rapidly becoming dark Hodge was in his office to receive the message. For him there had been no rest as he kept his finger on the hundreds of men scattered around trying to locate Cassell.

'Well, what's happened?' he asked Craymond, when at last he gained the Electro-Physical Laboratory.

'The very thing I'd been hoping for, though I had no accurate means of predicting it. Hodge, we're going to win! Cassell is going to fall into our hands like a ripe plum!'

'You hope! So far he's made an excellent job of giving us the slip.'

'So far, yes. But it won't go on. You must be aware of the reports that spurious cold light amongst the masses is dying out? In an hour of two it will be extinct. Once a false energy of that kind starts to dissipate it's no time before it's gone.'

'I've heard the reports, yes, but I — ' Hodge stopped and aimed a puzzled look. 'What are you getting at?'

'Answer me a question first. What's the latest news on Cassell?'

'We traced him as far as the city center, and then a body was found in an abandoned garage. The victim had died from electric shock, so plainly it was Cassell's work. After that we lost him. Then a woman by the name of Mary Lipscomb 'phoned in to say he had turned up at her place in the East End. Apparently she was once his girl friend. We rushed some men there. The woman's call came in following our broadcast warning, and obviously she was after the reward. Latest report is that she's dead with her head battered in and no sign of Cassell.'

'He might be anywhere, then?'

Hodge nodded moodily. 'We haven't picked his trail up again.'

'You will. Don't you understand, man? You've no work to do any more! In a few hours cold light of the spurious type will have faded from everybody who has it, and that's going to leave Cassell shining like a beacon light wherever he is. He cannot remain hidden forever, and the moment he is spotted he'll be nabbed. All the better if he doesn't know that cold light has faded from everybody but himself: he'll probably walk abroad from wherever he is, and become immediately visible. You'd better tip off the police in every part of the country to notify you the instant they spot him.'

'But can you guarantee that he alone will be glowing?' Hodge demanded. 'There'll be the hell of a mix-up if you're wrong.'

'I'm not,' Craymond replied flatly. 'I knew when I recently examined that man with spurious cold light emanation that it was only a question of time before the effect died out — but, as I said earlier, I could not predict when. Now I know. It has begun, and in the space of a few hours, maybe before dawn, every trace of it will have gone except from the possessor of the original 'ailment.' From then on Cassell will be the only man on Earth with cold light.'

Hodge began to move. 'Right! I'll advise all stations and let you know the moment anything happens.'

Craymond nodded and turned back to the inter-radio, which, by special arrangement, was giving him details of the spurious cold light failure at fifteen-minute intervals. By eleven o'clock he estimated that one half of the country's population had returned to normal. By midnight, three quarters. It was possible that by one or two in the morning only Sid Cassell would be left 'on view.'

Sid Cassell himself was quite unaware of the trend of events. He had succeeded in fitting himself out in a change of clothes, chiefly by visiting a small clothing store where, to judge from the proprietor, it was not even known yet that Mafeking had been relieved. After this, a meal in a back street dive, and then a train due south. In consequence, towards ten o'clock that evening, Sid arrived in the bar-room of the 'Sloping Shovel' public house, the haunt of villagers in a back-of-beyond region of Sussex.

There was a hush in the busy tap-room for a moment as Sid entered — and his appearance certainly gave occasion for it. He was wearing a heavy overcoat with the collar turned up, gloves, a soft hat, and a big scarf tied up to his eyes. Here came dark glasses. In one hand he carried a suitcase. Then the passing interest had gone and the hubbub of voices resumed.

Sid crossed to the bar-counter. 'Any chance of a room for tonight?' he asked the landlord.

'Well, now — ' Mine host reflected, then as he caught sight of Treasury notes in Sid's gloved hand his mood changed quickly. 'Yes, sir, I can fix you up, I think. Pay in advance; that's the rule. You'll be a commercial, I suppose?'

'Right. My car's broken down. I'll have

to stay for the night and move on tomorrow if the repairs are finished in time. Otherwise I may be here indefinitely.'

'I see. Having trouble with the teeth?'

Sid nodded. 'All the bottom ones out. I want to try and get some sleep. How much?'

The landlord told him. Sid paid, signed a grubby-looking register under the name of 'Hugh Brown' and then went up a rickety staircase behind the landlord's massive wife. She stopped on the corridor and threw open the door of one of the rooms.

'Here it is, sir.' She switched on the electric light.

'Thank you. It'll do fine,' Sid muttered, stepping past her. 'I'd like some supper brought up, please. Something pretty substantial. I'm hungry.'

'Yes, sir.' The woman turned to go and then hesitated. 'Substantial, sir, with your bottom teeth out?'

Sid muttered something to himself; then aloud, 'I'll try anyway. I'm sick of slops.'

The woman went and closed the door, listening in some wonder to the click of the key that followed it. She returned downstairs to her husband as he served behind the bar.

'Something queer about that fellow upstairs, Harry,' she muttered. 'I know if I'd had all my bottom teeth out I'd not forget it.'

'Meaning what?' Her husband served a pint briskly.

'Meaning he wants a substantial meal. Don't seem natural to me. Not natural, either, for him to keep his dark glasses on inside, less there's something queer about his eyes.'

'Forget it.' Harry gave a shrug. 'He's paid in advance an' it's no business of ours.'

His wife reflected for a moment, then with a shrug she went on her way into the domestic regions and prepared the meal for which Sid had asked. Meantime Sid was waiting in his room and having a surreptitious smoke. At the first sound on the door from the landlord's wife he was ready to pitch the cigarette into the ancient fireplace. It was difficult maneuvering a cigarette whilst wearing gloves.

Then at last there came the knock on the door. Sid made to whip the cigarette out of his mouth, but to his annoyance the paper had stuck to his lip. In consequence his gloved fingers whipped along the length of the cigarette and dragged off the glowing end. He crushed it between his gloved fingers and tossed the rest of the cigarette into the fireplace. Then he opened the door, carefully re-fixing his scarf in position as he did so.

'Very kind of you, I'm sure,' he said, as the woman moved to the table and set the tray down. 'Sorry to give you so much trouble.'

'No trouble, sir, believe me.' The woman straightened up and looked at him. 'I'm just puzzled how you're going to eat it. I've made the sandwiches soft as I can and taken off the crusts.' She stopped and looked about her quickly. 'Something burning in here. Smells like cloth.'

Sid could smell it, too, but he failed to observe anything, which was not surprising considering his dark glasses. He raised his hand to adjust them and the woman gave a gasp.

'It's your glove, sir! It's burning!'

Instantly Sid batted at his hand, knocking out the glowing strands which had evidently been smoldering since his accident with the cigarette. He gave a short laugh.

'Bad start I made with a cigarette,' he explained. 'My eyes are pretty poor, as you can see. Glad you noticed it. No damage done.'

'If — if you want anything more, sir, just call,' the woman said. 'Otherwise the tray will do in the morning.'

Then she went, with a baffled expression. Not that Sid could see it through his goggles. The moment she had gone he locked the door and then tugged the scarf from his face, tossing the glasses down after it. He looked at his glove. There was a fair hole in the wool. A thought crossed his mind, a grim one, then he dismissed it.

'What if she did?' he muttered. 'I'm not alone in this condition.'

Dismissing the incident he turned to

the supper and set about it ravenously. Meantime, the landlord's wife had arrived back downstairs, breathless with the speed of her descent.

'Now what?' her husband enquired curiously, eyeing her.

'It's — him!' she gasped out. 'Sidney Cassell!'

'Eh? Come off it — '

'I tell you it is! Nobody much left with that glowing effect now, is there? Said so on the news. Told all of us to watch for the cold light man. I tell you it's Sidney Cassell. He's got a hole in his glove and I saw his finger glowing where the hole was. Bright as a glow-worm it was.'

Her husband hesitated, looked towards the stairs, then glanced across to his nightly helper.

'Bill, nip over to Constable Ferrin's and tell him to come here. May be something important for him to deal with.'

'Okay.' Bill went off quickly. The landlord looked at his wife.

'Just act as if nothing's happened. If that muffled up blighter upstairs *is* Sidney

Cassell it's for the police to deal with, not us.'

Sid, up in his room, was entirely oblivious to the threat gathering around him, chiefly because he still was not aware that he alone of all men and women was the only one who glowed with uncanny radiance, his hands moving like phosphorescence itself as he ate his sandwiches and drank the beer. When he had finished he studied his phantasmagoric face for a moment or two in the mirror and smiled cynically; then he made preparations for retiring.

A thought struck him as he removed his collar and tie. Perhaps it would not be sensible to completely don a pyjama suit. He was wanted for murder and at any moment might have to make a dash for safety. So at last he lay down in shirt and trousers, the light switched off, his hands and face alone casting enough glow to illuminate the room. The sounds downstairs quieted gradually until presumably the night's business and clearing up was over.

He found himself wondering where this fantastic business was going to end. Had he really told the truth to Mary when he had said that eventually he would control a vast organization devoted to cold light? Or was he to spend the rest of his life as a hunted fugitive, as uncanny-looking a human being as ever walked the Earth?

Thus were his thoughts as he fell asleep. He was awakened again by a thunderous hammering on the bedroom door. Immediately he opened his eyes, shifting firefly hands on the coverlet He cleared his throat.

'Who is it?' he damanded sleepily.

'Police! Open up, Sidney Cassell, or we'll break the door down.'

Immediately Sid was completely awake. In one bound, following a preconceived move, he leapt from bed to window. Flinging it open he stared outside. He could see dim shapes, which looked like police cars, and the sounds of people's voices.

'There he is!'

'At the window there!'

'Stand back everybody!' commanded a voice in authority: then it addressed itself to Sid himself. 'Better give in, Cassell.

We've got the place surrounded.'

Sid's eyes narrowed. Once again his years of pylon climbing came to his rescue and with an adroit movement he swung out to the gutter of the ancient place and quickly twisted himself up onto the roof. Clearly visible because of his hands and face he sped up the roof itself and vanished over its apex. From the sounds below it was plain he had thrown plans for his capture into confusion.

Moving at top speed he dropped to a lower portico and from there to the rear yard. A chained dog raised hell. A constable came speeding out of the dark and then recoiled, stunned or dead, as Sid lashed out at him with a blazing fist. Another came and took a blow on the jaw that paralyzed him with shock. Without even a glance back Sid raced across the yard, vaulted the wall, and found himself a little way down the road from the pub's main entrance.

'Hey, there, Cassell!' came a shout, and he thought he recognized the voice of Dr. Craymond. 'Come here and you won't get hurt.'

'Like hell!' Sid muttered.

As he leapt up the grass bank at the side of the road, and so gained the field beyond, he began to struggle with his shirt. He succeeded finally, as he stumbled through grass and ditches, in forcing it over his head to partially hide the glow that was giving him away. But he had soon to drop it again as the need for air and enclosing warmth half smothered him.

Back among the police cars Dr. Craymond was nearly dancing with excitement and chagrin.

'Get him, you fools!' he yelled. '*Get him*! There he goes plain as a pillar of fire. But don't kill him. Rope him off somehow.'

'Come on!' Chief-Inspector Hodge snapped. 'We've got to get him!'

In a body, Dr. Craymond amongst them, the special detachment of men summoned from London — on the evidence of the village constable who had seen Sid asleep, through the bedroom window — went blundering up the grass bank in pursuit of the will-o'-the-wisps which marked Sid's blundering progress.

'To be hoped he doesn't fall into Barber Cleft,' panted the village constable, plugging along in the lead. 'It's a two hundred foot drop there into an old quarry working — '

'He *mustn't* fall into it!' Craymond shouted, nearly weeping at the thought. 'That man's worth millions. Millions!'

During this time, breathing harshly, Sid reached a rising stretch of ground and hurried up it, caring no longer whether his luminosity was betraying his whereabouts or not. He had only one thought: to escape the hounds of the law and science who were tearing after him in the background.

'Come back here!' came a faint cry from Dr. Craymond. 'Don't be an idiot, Cassell! I'll protect you against the law. You can't get away: we can follow you to the end of the country. You'll kill yourself if you're not careful. There's an old quarry around here somewhere.'

Sid hesitated for a moment, then branched off to the left. He was resolute that the law should not catch him, and equally resolute that his unhappy secret should not fall into the hands of the scientist who he was convinced had betrayed him.

On he ran, and still on. He reached the top of the rise and began to pelt down the opposite side: then suddenly he was racing into sheer space where the ground had disappeared and there was only the soundless rushing of the wind and headlong falling.

'My God, Barber Cleft!' shouted the village constable, the first to reach the top of the rise. 'I do believe he's fallen into it! No sign of him — '

'Search! Quickly!' Craymond came panting to the constable's side. 'Even if he has fallen in the cleft he may still be alive.'

'We'd better hurry,' Hodge said, and began to direct operations.

They found Sid an hour later, stone dead at the base of the quarry. Their difficulty was that they could not see him. There was no glow to betray his presence — only the lifeless clay half buried amidst ooze and slime.

'Well?' Hodge asked at last, peering at Dr. Craymond in the faint glow of the overworked flashlamps.

'It's finished.' Craymond's voice sounded like that of a father who had lost a first born. 'Whether he did it deliberately or not we shall never know, but he's dead. And with his death cold light has gone.' He made a restless movement. 'Oh, the crass idiocy of it all! One of the greatest secrets science has sought and it may never come again.'

There was a long silence; then Hodge said gruffly:

'All right, men, you can handle him. He's got no more electrical reaction. Let's get a rope around him. If we'd still had the death penalty, he'd have been due for a rope anyway.'

THE END

We do hope that you have enjoyed reading this large print book.

Did you know that all of our titles are available for purchase?

We publish a wide range of high quality large print books including:
Romances, Mysteries, Classics
General Fiction
Non Fiction and Westerns

Special interest titles available in large print are:
The Little Oxford Dictionary
Music Book, Song Book
Hymn Book, Service Book

Also available from us courtesy of Oxford University Press:
Young Readers' Dictionary
(large print edition)
Young Readers' Thesaurus
(large print edition)

For further information or a free brochure, please contact us at:
Ulverscroft Large Print Books Ltd.,
The Green, Bradgate Road, Anstey,
Leicester, LE7 7FU, England.
Tel: (00 44) **0116 236 4325**
Fax: (00 44) **0116 234 0205**

6